Linda Lael Miller has made the Western frontier her own special place, and never more so than in this heartwarming new series that brings four women west to share an inheritance—2,500 acres of timber and high-country grassland called Primrose Creek.

In this wonderful new series, four cousins discover the dangers and the joys, the hardship and the beauty, of frontier life. And each, in her own way, finds a love that will last an eternity. Join with the McQuarry women in a special celebration of the love, courage, and family ties that made the West great.

Four special women. Four extraordinary stories.

THE WOMEN OF PRIMROSE CREEK

BRIDGET

CHRISTY

SKYE

Praise for Linda Lael Miller's bestselling series

SPRINGWATER SEASONS

"A DELIGHTFUL AND DELICIOUS MINI-SERIES. . . . *Rachel* will charm you, enchant you, delight you, and quite simply hook you. . . . *Miranda* is a sensual marriage-of-convenience tale guaranteed to warm your heart all the way down to your toes. . . . The warmth that spreads through *Jessica* is captivating. . . . The gentle beauty of the tales and the delightful, warmhearted characters bring a slice of Americana straight onto readers' 'keeper' shelves. Linda Lael Miller's miniseries is a gift to treasure." —*Romantic Times*

"This hopeful tale is . . . infused with the sensuality that Miller is known for." —*Booklist*

"All the books in this collection have the Linda Lael Miller touch." —*Affaire de Coeur*

"Nobody brings the folksiness of the Old West to life better than Linda Lael Miller." —*BookPage*

"Another warm, tender story from the ever-so-talented pen of one of this genre's all-time favorites." —*Rendezvous*

"Miller . . . create[s] a warm and cozy love story." —*Publishers Weekly*

Books by Linda Lael Miller

Banner O'Brien	Pirates
Corbin's Fancy	Knights
Memory's Embrace	My Outlaw
My Darling Melissa	The Vow
Angelfire	Two Brothers
Desire and Destiny	Springwater
Fletcher's Woman	Springwater Seasons series:
Lauralee	Rachel
Moonfire	Savannah
Wanton Angel	Miranda
Willow	Jessica
Princess Annie	A Springwater Christmas
The Legacy	One Wish
Taming Charlotte	The Women of Primrose Creek series:
Yankee Wife	Bridget
Daniel's Bride	Christy
Lily and the Major	Skye
Emma and the Outlaw	Megan
Caroline and the Raider	

Linda Lael Miller

The Women
of Primrose Creek

MEGAN

SONNET BOOKS
New York London Toronto Sydney Singapore

This book is a work of fiction. Names, characters, places and incidents are products of the author's imagination or are used fictitiously. Any resemblance to actual events or locales or persons, living or dead, is entirely coincidental.

An *Original* Publication of POCKET BOOKS

A Sonnet Book published by
POCKET BOOKS, a division of Simon & Schuster Inc.
1230 Avenue of the Americas, New York, NY 10020

ISBN: 0-671-04247-5

First Sonnet Books printing August 2000

10 9 8 7 6 5 4 3 2 1

SONNET BOOKS and colophon are trademarks of
Simon & Schuster Inc.

Front cover illustration by Robert Hunt

Printed in the U.S.A.

For all my loyal readers,
with gratitude and love

MEGAN

Chapter

1

∞

Primrose Creek, Nevada
June 1870

Dust billowed around the stagecoach as Megan McQuarry stepped down, grasping the skirts of her black-and-white striped silk dress in one hand. She'd been traveling for several endless, bone-jolting days, but she'd taken care with her appearance all along the way. She'd washed whenever the opportunity arose, which was seldom enough, and done her best to keep her auburn hair tidy and her hat firmly affixed, at just the proper angle. She was penniless, a miserable failure, with nothing but a trunk full of missed cues and frayed dreams to show for two years on her own, but she still had the formidable McQuarry pride.

She had returned to Primrose Creek in defeat, there was no denying that, but not without a certain bittersweet sense of homecoming. Coming back meant seeing her sister Christy again, after all, and her two cousins, Bridget and Skye. They'd had the good sense to stay put, Christy and the others, and now they had homes, husbands, children. Their lives were busy and full, bright with color and passion; she knew that from the letters Skye had written while she was away, always pleading with her to return to Primrose Creek.

She sighed and squared her aching shoulders, bracing herself for what lay ahead. Her kin would welcome her, she knew; they'd enfold her in laughter and love, include her in their doings, defend her fiercely against the inevitable snubs and gossip her return would arouse. But they would be angry, too, and confused, for she had left suddenly, leaving behind only a brief note of explanation.

She shaded her eyes as she looked up at the coach driver, who was unstrapping her secondhand trunk and getting ready to toss it down at her feet. She hoped he wouldn't expect any sort of recompense, because she'd used the last of her funds the day before, to purchase a bowl of stew at a way station. She hadn't eaten since.

"Be careful with that, please," she said, indicating the trunk. *It's all I have.* And it was. She'd long since sold her share of the prime timber- and grassland left to the four McQuarry women to some rancher, through a banker and a lawyer, and now she would be the poor relation, beholden for every bite of bread and bolt of calico she got until the day she went to her final rest. If only that were the worst of it, she thought.

"Yes, ma'am," the driver answered, and let the trunk fall with an unceremonious clunk onto the wooden sidewalk, raising grit from between the boards. Megan would have taken off some of the fellow's hide if she hadn't been so weary, so hungry, and so utterly disconsolate.

She was just reaching for the trunk's battered handle, meaning to drag the monstrosity across the road to her brother-in-law's office—Zachary Shaw was the town marshal—when a large leather-gloved hand eased her own aside. She looked up, expecting to see Zachary, or perhaps Trace Qualtrough, Bridget's husband, or Jake Vigil, who had married Skye around the time of Megan's flight. Instead, she found herself gazing into a stranger's face; a man with tanned skin, wheat-colored hair, and periwinkle-blue eyes grinned down at her. His teeth were sturdy and white as a new snowfall gleaming under morning sunlight.

He tugged at the brim of his weathered leather hat. "You planning to stay on here at Primrose Creek, ma'am? I do hope you aren't just passing through— that would be a sore disappointment."

Megan was used to sweet-talking men, God knew, and good-looking ones, too, but there was something about this one that caused her breath to catch as surely as if she'd just tumbled headfirst into an ice-cold mountain stream. All her senses, dulled by trouble and the long trip from San Francisco, leaped instantly to life, and she knew by looking into the man's eyes that he'd taken note of her reactions to him, and been pleased.

She was furious, with him and with herself. If there was one thing she didn't need, it was a man, however intriguing and fair to look upon that man might happen to be. "Thank you," she said stiffly, "but I'm sure my brother-in-law will collect my baggage—"

The stranger looked around pointedly. "I don't see anybody headed this way," he observed in a cheerful tone of voice. "I'm Webb Stratton, just in case you're worried that we haven't had a proper introduction."

The name slammed into Megan's middle like a barrel rolling downhill. She waited to regain her equilibrium, then put out a slightly tremulous hand. "Megan McQuarry," she said, by reflex. It was nearly too much to bear, that this man of all people should be the first person she encountered upon her homecoming. She had to admit there was a certain ironic justice in it, though.

His grin broadened in apparent recognition, and he pumped her hand, failing to notice, it would seem, that all the blood had drained from her face and she was unsteady on her feet. Mr. Stratton had bought her land, the land she should never, *ever* have sold. She cringed to think what Granddaddy would have said about such a betrayal.

"Well, now, Miss McQuarry," said Mr. Stratton, still at ease and still gripping her hand. Megan felt a grudging gratitude, for between her empty stomach and her many regrets, she wasn't entirely sure she could stand on her own. "I know your family. They're neighbors of mine."

A flush climbed Megan's cheeks. Skye, always her closest friend as well as her beloved cousin, was likely to be understanding where Megan's many mistakes were concerned, but Bridget and Christy would have an opinion or two when it came to the sale of the land. Especially when they found out how she'd been hoodwinked by a no-good man. She opened her mouth, closed it again.

"My wagon's right over there," Mr. Stratton said,

nodding to indicate the end of the street. Only then did he release her hand, and she marveled that she hadn't pulled away long since. "I'd be happy to drive you and your baggage out to Primrose Creek."

She was not the sort of woman who accepted favors from men she had never met before, but Mr. Stratton wasn't exactly a stranger, and Primrose Creek certainly wasn't San Francisco. "Very well," she said. "Thank you."

She had time to consider the rashness of her decision while Mr. Stratton went to fetch the wagon. It was drawn by two well-bred paint geldings, Megan noted as she watched him approach; as did everyone else in her family, she appreciated fine horseflesh.

Stratton jumped easily to the ground, after setting the brake lever with a thrust of one leg, and Megan's attention shifted back to him, taking in his tall frame, broad shoulders, and cattleman's garb of denim trousers, chambray shirt, and buckskin vest. His hat was as worn as his boots, and, unlike most of the men Megan knew, he did not carry a gun.

Megan straightened her spine and studiously ignored the curious looks coming at her from all directions. She could almost hear the speculations—*Isn't that the McQuarry girl? The one who ran away to become an actress? She has her share of brass, doesn't she, coming back here, expecting to live among decent people, just as if nothing had happened . . .*

The sound of her trunk landing in the rear of Mr. Stratton's wagon brought her back to the present moment with a snap. He tugged his hat brim in a cordial greeting to two plump matrons passing by on the sidewalk. "Last I heard," he remarked, "it was considered impolite to stare." Caught, the women puffed their bosoms like prairie hens and trundled away. She could almost see their feathers bristling.

Megan couldn't help smiling with amusement, as tired and discouraged as she was. Webb—*Webb?*—was grinning again as he handed her up into the wagon box. He rounded the buckboard, climbed up beside her, took the reins in his hands, and released the brake lever. The rig lurched forward.

"Seems you're the topic of some serious speculation," he observed dryly as they reached the end of the street and left the busy little town behind for the timbered countryside.

Megan heaved a soft sigh. Her smile had already slipped away, and her hands were knotted in her lap, fingers tangled in the strings of her empty handbag. "Surely you've realized, Mr. Stratton—"

"Webb," he interrupted kindly.

"Webb," Megan conceded, with some impatience. She started again. "Surely you've realized that the land you bought last year was mine."

He regarded the road thoughtfully, though Megan suspected he could have made the journey over that track in a sound sleep. "Well," he allowed, after some time, "yes. I reckon I figured that out right away." He glanced at her, sidelong, and a sweet shiver went through her. "Does it matter?"

She sat up even straighter and raised her chin. "I did not like parting with my property," she said stiffly. "Circumstances demanded that I do so." That wasn't his fault, of course, but knowing it didn't change the way she felt. "Perhaps we could work out terms of some sort, and I could buy it back."

Again, he took the time to consider her words. It annoyed her; he was well aware that she was in suspense—she could see that in his eyes—but apparently he didn't mind letting her squirm awhile. "Couldn't do that," he said finally. "I built myself a house there. A good barn and corral, too."

Megan bit her upper lip and willed the hot tears stinging behind her eyes to recede. It was going to kill her to see someone else living on her share of Granddaddy's bequest, but she had no one to thank but herself. She'd been so gullible, believing Davy Trent's pretty promises the way she had, and she was more ashamed of her brief association with that thieving polecat than anything she'd ever done. She learned some valuable lessons, but they'd come at a high price.

McQuarry that she was, the land as much a part of her as her pulse and the marrow of her bones, she had nonetheless made the sale, handed over the profits so that she and Davy could buy a small ranch near Stockton and be married. Instead, he'd swindled her, left her alone and humiliated, with barely a penny to her name.

"They expecting you? Your people, I mean?" Webb's voice was gentle and quiet, and the teasing light that had been lurking in his eyes was gone.

She swallowed hard, shook her head. "It'll be a surprise, I think," she said. "My showing up now, I mean."

He took off his hat, replaced it again. The gesture reminded Megan of her granddaddy, Gideon McQuarry. He'd had the same habit; it was a sign that he was thinking. "They'll be glad to see you, you know," Webb ventured.

Megan bit her lip for a moment, in order to recover a little. "They'll take me in," she said, very softly. It didn't seem necessary to point out that taking somebody in was a world away from welcoming them. Forgiving them.

"You were an actress," he said, with no inflection at all.

She sat up a little straighter, shot him a fiery glance. "Yes."

"What sort of roles did you play?"

She was taken aback by the question. There was no mockery in his tone or manner, and nothing to indicate that he considered her loose by virtue of her profession, as many men did. "Shakespearean, mostly," she allowed. "Ophelia. Kate in *The Taming of the Shrew.*"

He chuckled. "I don't see you as Ophelia. Just by looking at you, I'd say you weren't the type to lose your mind over a man. Any man. Now, the part of Kate, on the other hand—I can imagine that right enough."

Megan was amazed, not so much by his statements—frank to the point of being downright forward though they were—as by his knowledge of the Bard's plays. In her experience, most cowboys found them incomprehensible, if they paid any notice at all. Somewhat haltingly, she told him how she'd favored the role of Ophelia, simply because of the challenge it represented, being so at variance with her own nature. She even admitted that she would miss the stage.

Webb listened and nodded once or twice, but he offered no further comment. Shortly thereafter, the rooftop of Christy and Zachary's house came into view. Once an abandoned Indian lodge, with leaky animal hides for a roof, it had been renovated into one of the finest places around, and it was a very happy place, according to Skye's newsy letters. Joseph, Megan's nephew, was two already, and his baby sister, Margaret, was approaching her first birthday.

Megan yearned to lay eyes on those children, to feel Christy's arms around her, to be a part of the clan once again. She wished she'd never left home in the first place, of course, but hindsight was always clear as creek water. Besides, she'd learned a great deal during her brief career, learned to project confidence even when she was terrified. And God knew, she'd learned something about men—specifically Davy Trent.

Christy came out into the dooryard, hearing the noise of the wagon, shading her eyes from the late-morning sunshine. Caney—dear Caney—was soon beside her, gazing their way, but Megan could tell nothing of her mood from her countenance. Caney Blue, a black woman, had worked for Gideon and Rebecca McQuarry for many years. When the farm in Virginia's Shenandoah Valley was sold for taxes after the war, and Megan and Christy, fresh from England, had set out to claim their one-quarter shares of a twenty-five hundred-acre tract known as Primrose Creek, Caney had come along.

Christy's face kindled with joy as she recognized her sister. She clapped one hand over her mouth, caught up her skirts with the other, and ran toward the wagon, limber as a girl. "Megan!" she cried.

Megan was down from the wagon box and flinging

herself into Christy's arms within the space of a heart-beat. They clung to each other, the pair of sisters, laughing and crying, while Caney stood back, smiling. Webb Stratton unloaded the trunk without a word and carried it into the house.

"Look at you!" Christy cried, beaming, as she gripped Megan's upper arms in both hands and held her away. "You're beautiful!"

Megan didn't feel beautiful, she felt broken and soiled, used and discarded, and her throat was clogged with emotion. She couldn't speak but merely hugged Christy again, hard.

Webb came out of the house again, climbed back into his buckboard.

"Thank you," Christy told him, as warmly as if he'd gone out and searched the world for Megan and then brought her back to Primrose Creek like a prodigal daughter. "Oh, thank you."

He merely nodded, touched Megan lightly with that wildflower-blue gaze of his, and set the team in motion again, the buckboard jostling along the high grassy bank overlooking the sparkling creek.

"Where on earth have you been?" Christy demanded good-naturedly, linking her arm with Megan's and steering her toward the house. In the doorway, a little boy with bright blond hair looked on, a tiny dark-haired girl at his side.

"I'd like to know that myself," Caney put in, keeping pace. Her beautiful dark brown eyes had narrowed slightly.

So Skye had kept her promise, Megan thought, and never divulged her whereabouts. Perhaps she hadn't even told the family she was receiving an occasional letter from the McQuarry-gone-astray.

"Just about everywhere," Megan admitted, longing for sleep and tea and a nice, hot bath. Tears of happiness slipped down her cheeks as she reached the children and knelt before them, heedless of her skirts. They studied her curiously, Joseph his father in miniature, Margaret a re-creation of Christy, with a chubby forefinger caught in her mouth. "I'm your Aunt Megan," she said.

Joseph put out his hand in solemn greeting, small as he was, and Megan shook it. Margaret clung to her brother's shirt and edged shyly backward, out of reach.

Megan smiled and got to her feet.

Christy slipped an arm around her waist, and they entered the cool, fragrant interior of the house. It was full of light, and the floors shone with wax. Curtains danced at the open windows, and framed watercolors, probably Christy's own work, graced the walls. Hard to believe it was the same place, Megan thought, where they'd made their meals in a fire pit and slept on bales of hay shoved together for beds, those first weeks after their arrival at Primrose Creek several years before.

"I see you've met Webb Stratton," Christy said, her tone a shade less genial as she went to the wood box next to the shining cookstove and began feeding the fire to heat water for tea. Suddenly, there was a snappish tension in the air, like the metallic charge that precedes a violent storm. Perhaps Skye hadn't betrayed Megan's confidences, but the family couldn't help knowing that she'd done the unthinkable and sold a portion of the land. They would hold that against her, as they would the worry she had caused them.

"Yes," Megan replied, with a half-hearted stab at dignity. She was unpinning her hat, removing it, setting it aside atop a sturdy pinewood table. No doubt Trace had built that piece of furniture, as he had many others, in his workshop across the creek. He and Bridget had made their home in a sprawling log house, and, at last report, they'd had four children, counting Noah, Bridget's son by her first marriage.

Joseph and Margaret were hovering at a safe distance, watching Megan as though they expected her to turn a back flip or sprout wings and fly around the room. She smiled at them before taking a chair at the round oak table where the family took their meals.

"Come along with Caney, now," Caney said, gathering the children and shooing them toward one of the bedrooms. "Last time I looked, you two had left your toys scattered from here to kingdom come." No fool, Caney. She'd probably sensed the shift in the emotional weather even before Christy and Megan had.

"We were surprised," Christy said, with a false brightness that was all too familiar to Megan, busying herself at the stove, "when you sold your share of the land to a complete stranger."

Megan twisted her fingers together. "I'm sorry," she said.

"Sorry," Christy echoed. She stood in profile, high color in her cheeks, her spine straight as a store-bought hoe handle. "You're *sorry*."

Megan sighed. She had expected just such a recep-

MEGAN *13*

tion, but that didn't make the confrontation any easier. "Yes," she said wearily.

Christy slammed the tea kettle down hard on the gleaming surface of her huge iron and chrome cookstove. "You might have written."

Megan looked down at her hands, twisted together in her lap. "I did write," she said, very quietly. "To Skye. I asked her not to tell you where I was."

Christy paused, dabbed at her eyes with the hem of her blue-and-white checked apron. "Well, she certainly respected your wishes." She straightened again and drew a deep breath in a typical bid to regain control of her emotions. "That's something, I suppose." She turned, at last, and faced her sister. "Oh, Megan, how could you? How could you leave us to worry like that?"

Megan let out her breath; until then, she hadn't realized she was holding it. "I was ashamed," she said.

Christy looked stunned, as though she'd expected any answer in the world save that one. "Ashamed?" she echoed, her brow knitted prettily above her charcoal eyes. "I don't understand."

Megan forced herself to hold her sister's gaze, though she longed to look away. She could feel her face taking flame. "I was—I made a stupid mistake."

Christy crossed the room, the tea-making paraphernalia forgotten in the kitchen, and sank into a chair facing Megan. Her eyes glimmered with tears. "Oh, Megan, surely you didn't think anything you could have done—"

Megan swallowed hard. "There was a man," she said, and just uttering the words was like coughing with sharp stones caught in her throat. "I met him not—not long after I joined that first theater troupe, in Virginia City."

Christy reached across the tabletop and took one of Megan's hands in both her own. In that instant, Megan knew she could have confided in her elder sister and found understanding, but the awareness had come too late. The damage was already done. "Go on," she said, very softly.

"His name was—is—Davy Trent. He—well, I thought he was entirely another sort of man—like Zachary, or Trace, or Skye's Jake—but I was wrong."

Christy simply waited, though her grasp tightened slightly.

Megan sniffled, raised her chin. She had come this far. She would see this through. Make a fresh start, right here among these people who loved her even when she disappointed them. "I was such a fool." Megan raised her free hand to her mouth for a long moment, then forced herself to go on. Christy was silent, pale. "He—he said we were going to be married. There was a ranch for sale—we were supposed to buy it, live there—"

"But?" Christy prompted.

"He cheated me. I sold the property here at Primrose Creek, and instead of making the down payment, like we'd planned, and going through with the wedding, Davy took the proceeds and lit out." In her head, she paraphrased an old saying of her granddaddy's. *A fool and her money are soon parted.*

Christy slid forward to the edge of her chair and gathered Megan into her arms, held her. "How terrible."

"I wanted to come home then, but I was too embarrassed, and I didn't have stage fare," Megan went on when the brief embrace had ended. "I waited tables and scrubbed floors until I'd saved enough to leave."

Christy sighed. "You should have wired us that you were in trouble," she said. "Zachary and I would have come for you ourselves."

Megan shook her head. Her eyes felt hot and dry; it would have been a relief to weep, but she couldn't. "I'm here now," she said.

"And you can make a brand-new start," Christy said gently. She smoothed a stray tendril of hair back from Megan's temple. "Everything will be all right, Megan."

Megan's throat felt thick, and she dared not attempt to say any more before she'd had time to compose herself. She simply nodded again.

Water from the tea kettle began to spill, sizzling, onto the stovetop, and both women ignored it. "Are you sure he's gone for good?" Christy pressed. "This scoundrel who fleeced you, I mean? Maybe Zachary could find him, get back your money, at least—"

Megan gave a bitter chuckle, shook her head. "He's long gone," she said.

"No doubt that's for the best," Christy said, and got up briskly to finish brewing the tea.

"Tell me about Webb Stratton," Megan heard herself say.

Christy was bustling busily about the kitchen. A pretty frown creased her forehead. "I don't know much about him," she said, with plain regret. "He's from somewhere up north, Montana, I think, though he told Zachary he'd been drifting awhile before he settled here. And Trace says he knows more about ranching than most anybody else in the high country." A sudden smile lit her face. "He's unmarried, you know. Webb, I mean. He lives in that big house all by himself."

Megan knew exactly what Christy was thinking and gave her a narrow look. "I'm not interested," she said.

Christy was undaunted. In fact, she acted as if Megan hadn't spoken at all. "I guess if we had to part with any portion of Granddaddy's land, it could have gone to somebody a lot worse than Webb Stratton."

Megan felt a slight but dizzying flip in the pit of her stomach every time she heard the man's name. She stiffened a little, in an effort to brace herself against her own susceptibilities. "I asked him to sell the tract back to me," she said. "He refused."

"I'm not surprised," Christy acknowledged. "He's got a good two-story house and a fine barn built. Fences, too, and a well. He owns another thousand acres besides. Both Trace and Zachary agree that they wouldn't sell out, either, if they were in his shoes."

"They tried to buy the place?"

"No," Christy allowed, bringing a tray to the table, "but they discussed the matter at some length, and on more than one occasion." There were cookies and dried apricots on a china plate Megan remembered from their mother's table, and the familiar flowered teapot steamed with the fragrance of orange pekoe. Megan went lightheaded for a moment, and her hand shook visibly as she reached for a piece of fruit.

Christy noticed immediately and poured tea for her sister. Then, while Megan was still grappling with the weakness her hunger had brought on, Christy returned to the pantry and fetched cheese, bread, and fresh butter. Mercifully, she left Megan to eat in peace, laying a hand lightly on her shoulder as she passed, and went to prepare a bath and a bed.

Megan ate as much as she dared and allowed herself to be led into the spare bedroom, where Caney and Christy gently divested her of her clothes and helped her into a copper tub filled with warm water. She was silent while Caney washed her hair and Christy laid out towels, scented powder, and a clean nightgown.

After the bath, Megan dried herself, used a generous amount of talcum, pulled on the gown, and crawled between blissfully clean linen sheets. For the first time in almost two years, she slept soundly, and without fear.

All the McQuarry women were beautiful, Webb reminded himself that afternoon while he worked, sweating under a shirt, buckskin breeches, and a heavy leather apron, at the forge behind his barn. To his way of thinking, it shouldn't have surprised him to find out that Megan, with her coppery hair and clover-green eyes, surpassed them all.

He threw more wood onto the fire and worked the bellows with hard pumping motions of both arms. Shoeing horses, herding and branding cattle, riding fence lines, pitching hay—all of it was hard work, and Webb reveled in it. At night, when he stretched out on that narrow bed of his and closed his eyes, he sank to a place in his mind where neither dreams nor nightmares could reach, and as soon as he woke up, the whole cycle began all over again.

He frowned as he thrust a hard metal shoe into the

fire with pinchers and held it steady while it softened enough to yield to hammer blows on the anvil. Megan McQuarry had staked out a place in his thoughts and commenced to homesteading there, it seemed, for he couldn't seem to stop imagining the scent of her skin, the spirited light in her eyes, the inviting slender shape of her body. Until that morning, in town, she'd been a name on a deed to him and nothing more, but now that he'd met her, seen how proud she was, heard her talk about the plays she'd been in and the places she'd traveled, he'd gotten a real sense of her intelligence, her dignity, and the innate strength he suspected she didn't even know she had. He'd sat there beside her, on the seat of his buckboard, just listening, his thigh touching hers, and, well, something had changed.

He wrenched the shoe from the fire, laid it on the anvil, and began to strike it hard, metal ringing against metal. On and on he worked, firing and refiring, hammering and rehammering, until the shape suited. Occasionally, he thrust the shoe into a vat of water and blinked in the hissing cloud of steam that arose around him like a veil.

He was holding the pinto mare's right rear hoof in one hand and nailing a shoe into place with the other when Trace Qualtrough rode up on his newest acquisition, a dapple-gray stallion he'd bought off a horse trader down south someplace, and swung down from the saddle.

"Stratton," he said, by way of a greeting, tugging at the brim of his beat-up leather hat. A man as prosperous as Trace could have afforded any kind of hat he happened to fancy, but he seemed partial to that one—

in all the time he'd known him, Webb had never seen his neighbor wear another.

Webb nodded. "Afternoon," he said. He knew what the visit was about—he and Trace were good friends, but they were also busy men, not much given to chin-wagging sessions in the middle of the day—so there was no need to ask. Now that Megan was home from her travels, the McQuarry women and their assorted husbands would be wanting to buy back the land.

He finished driving in the last short nail, squatted to make sure the shoe wouldn't throw off the mare's balance, then straightened to his full height. He gave the pinto a swat on the flank, and she nickered and trotted off to find herself a patch of good grass.

"We'll give you a fair price," Trace said. He wasn't one to make a short story long, and that was one of the things Webb liked about him.

He shook his head. "I mean to stay right here," he said.

Trace took in the sturdy log house, the grass and timber, the cattle and horses grazing nearby. "I don't reckon I can blame you," he replied with a sigh of resignation. "Had to try, though."

Webb nodded. He knew all about trying, even when the odds were bad. Most westerners did.

"Bridget wants you to come to supper tomorrow night," Trace went on. "It's a celebration, 'cause Megan's home."

Webb knew he should refuse—common sense told him he ought to keep his distance from the redheaded Miss McQuarry, at least until he could get his impulses under control—but a neighbor's hospitality was something to be respected, and, anyway, he relished the prospect of woman-cooked food and some polite company. "I'd be pleased to pay a visit," he said.

Trace nodded. "She'll be setting the table about the time the evening chores are done, I reckon," he replied. Then he got back on his horse and, one hand raised briefly in farewell, rode away.

Webb watched him out of sight, then went down to the creek to wash. He'd get the stock fed early the next night and head into town for a real, hot-water bath upstairs at Diamond Lil's. Might even get his hair barbered and put on his Sunday suit, he reflected, and grinned to himself. The McQuarrys weren't the sort to give up easily, and if they couldn't get the land back one way, they'd try another. He wouldn't have put it past Bridget, Christy, and Skye to throw him and Megan together at every opportunity, hoping there would be a marriage.

Kneeling on the rocky bank of Primrose Creek, he splashed his face with icy water, then the back of his neck, and while the effort washed away some of the sweat and soot, it did nothing to cool the swift heat that had risen like a tide in his blood. He sure as hell wasn't going to marry into *that* outfit—he liked his women a little less opinionated—but the idea of sharing a bed with Megan McQuarry possessed him like a demon fever.

He took off his apron and shirt, drenched his chest, back, and arms with more water. Maybe he shouldn't have been so quick to accept Trace's invite to supper, he reflected, but since the deed was done, he couldn't see dwelling on regrets. He stood, snatched up his discarded clothing, and turned to head for the house.

The place was big but sparsely furnished, and entering the kitchen by way of the side door, Webb was struck yet again by the emptiness of the place. He hoped to marry one day and fill the rooms with kids, but for the moment he had to be content with his own company and that of his big yellow dog, Augustus. He still thought of his brother's wife, Eleanor, more often than he'd like, and of the children she might have given him, but she was up in Montana on the Stratton family ranch, the Southern Star, and she was likely to stay there.

He poured himself a cup of lukewarm coffee, stewing on the back of the stove since breakfast, took a sip, and winced. He wondered what kind of cook Megan McQuarry was, and then chuckled. Somehow, he couldn't picture her brewing coffee, let alone frying up a chicken or stirring a pot of oatmeal. Something had taken the starch right out of her—that was plain from her countenance and the bruised expression in her eyes—but like as not, she wouldn't stay at Primrose Creek for long, once she got her wind back. She wasn't the sort to settle down in one place; as soon as a troupe of show people passed within fifty miles, she'd take to the trail.

Webb's good spirits faded a little. He tossed the coffee into the cast-iron sink with a grimace of disgust and headed for the inside stairway.

His room, one of three sizable chambers, had a fireplace for cold nights, but the bed was nothing more than a cot, like the ones out in the bunkhouse, dragged up close to the hearth and covered with rumpled sheets and an old quilt. Just looking at it deepened his loneliness; he'd have to put in five or six more hours of work if he expected to sleep that night. There was always whiskey, of course, not to mention the friendly women who worked at Lil's, but he was in no mood for either, damn the luck.

He changed his clothes, went back out to the barn, and began the process of mucking out stalls with a pitchfork. By the time he finished, the sun had set. He entered the house again, dished up some of the beans he'd been working on for several days, and made himself eat. Then, figuring the grub had run its course, he carried the kettle outside and scraped the contents into a blue enamel dishpan with rusted edges.

Augustus meandered over to lap up his supper, and Webb smiled, patting the animal's hairy head. Bad planning on his part, he thought. The dog would have to sleep in the barn.

Chapter

2

$\mathcal{M}$egan awoke with the first twittering of the birds and took a few moments to orient herself to her surroundings. She was home, she thought, with relief—not sharing a bed in a second-rate hotel with two other actresses or freezing on a hard bench in the back of some shoddy saloon or show house. Not carrying trays in a dining hall or scouring a filthy floor on her hands and knees. She drew a deep breath of thin, pure high-country air and let it out slowly. She was home.

She arose, washed her face at the basin on the table next to the window, then wound her already-braided hair into a coronet and donned the only really proper dress she owned, a blue-and-white flowered cotton with a modest collar trimmed in narrow eyelet. When she slipped out of her room, at the rear of the house, she found Caney already at the stove, building up the fire. Gauzy rays of pinkish sunlight seeped through the eastern windows and made glowing pools on the hardwood floors.

"I figured I'd make up some oatmeal and sausage," Caney said, and the quiet coolness of her tone injured Megan a little, for the other woman might have been speaking to an interloper instead of an old friend. "Zachary likes a good meal in the morning. Something that'll stick to his ribs."

Megan nodded, a little shyly, keeping her distance. "Is there anything I can do to help?"

Caney set a skillet on the heat with a ringing thump. "Yes'um, there is," she said with just the slightest snap. "You can sit yourself down there at that table and not get underfoot."

The words were not amicable ones, but they were familiar, and for that reason alone they reassured Megan, however slightly. She drew back a chair and sat, for no sensible person took an argument with Caney Blue lightly, not even the four McQuarry women. "I want to explain—"

Caney held up one hand. "No, miss. I won't hear no 'explanations.' All I want to know is, you gonna stay here at Primrose Creek where you belong, or go runnin' off again, leavin' us all to wonder and fret over you?"

Megan lowered her head, raised it again. "I mean to stay," she said.

Caney regarded her in silence for a seemingly endless interval, then went back to her cooking. Zachary wandered in from the master bedroom, yawning expansively, his fair hair sleep-rumpled. He was wearing trousers, a button-up undershirt, suspenders, and boots. He nodded a cordial greeting to the ladies, ambled over to the wash stand by the back door, and squinted into the little mirror affixed to the wall. With a sigh of resignation, he bent to splash his face at the basin, then whipped up a lather with his soap cup and brush, and began the morning ritual of shaving. By nightfall, Megan knew, he would have to go through the whole process again, and she found herself wondering idly whether it was the same for Webb Stratton.

Just the thought of Stratton attending to such an intimate and implicitly masculine function, ordinary as it was, made Megan feel as though a half-dozen grasshoppers were playing jump rope in the pit of her stomach. She blushed and looked down at her hands.

"Trace spoke to Webb while you were resting yesterday," Zachary said, already wielding the blade. "About selling back the land. He won't budge."

Caney offered no comment, but it was plain that she was listening. A part of the family, she was privy to pretty much everything that went on in the three households.

Megan nodded. "I know," she said.

Zachary looked back at her, over one shoulder, his face still half covered in foam, the blade in one hand. His grin was quick and boyish, and, for an instant, she envied Christy the passionate, unconditional love he felt for her. Like Trace Qualtrough and Jake Vigil, he was devoted to his wife and family, and he didn't have any compunctions about letting the world know it.

"We've got plenty of room right here," he said. "Like as not, things will work themselves out, if you just stick around."

She blinked a little, touched by the assurance that there was still a place for her at Primrose Creek. She guessed that Zachary and Christy and all the rest of them expected her to take to her heels again at the first sign of difficulty. "I don't want to be a burden to you and Christy," she said. "I won't."

"Burden," Caney scoffed under her breath, tending to the fresh and fragrant sausage sizzling in a large black skillet.

Zachary grinned again and went back to shaving.

He had already finished eating and headed for town, wearing his badge and a well-used .45, when Christy appeared, clad in a lavender morning gown, her dark hair wound into a single thick plait, her cream-colored skin aglow with rest, good health, and some sweet, private secret. She made Megan think of an exotic night orchid, blooming in moonlight, folding back into a dignified bud by day. Joseph and little Margaret were close behind their mother, sleepy and serious in their flannel nightshirts and bare feet.

Megan's heart swelled with affection just to look at the children, her very own niece and nephew. Regret for all she'd missed seared the back of her throat, and she had to swallow hard before she could manage a hoarse good morning.

Christy paused as she passed, leaned down to kiss the top of her sister's head, and then went over to shoo Caney away from the sink, where she was washing dishes. "Go and sit down this instant," Christy told her friend.

To Megan's surprise, Caney obeyed and allowed Christy to serve her coffee and then breakfast. The children took their seats at the table, too, and tucked into bowls of hot oatmeal laced with fresh cream and molasses.

"Do you go to school?" Megan asked, gazing at Joseph. Although he had his father's coloring, she could see Christy clearly in the set of his jaw and the level, steady look in his eyes.

"I'm too little," he said. "But I can read. I can ride, too. I've got a pony."

Megan smiled. "My goodness," she said.

"I might not ever go to school," he added after considerable rumination.

"I beg to differ," Christy stated lightly, joining the rest of them at the table and taking a delicate sip from her coffee. "You will *most certainly* go to school, Joseph Shaw."

He frowned. "I want to be Pa's deputy. I figure I won't have time for school."

Christy hid a smile, but Megan caught a glimpse of it, dancing in her gray eyes. "What use is a deputy with no education?" she asked reasonably. "Now, finish your breakfast. You have chores to do, unless I'm mistaken."

"Chickens to feed," Joseph told Megan importantly.

"And I could use a little help weeding that garden," Caney announced.

Megan made a show of pushing up her sleeves. "I might as well attend to that," she said. "Make myself useful around here."

A brief silence ensued, and Joseph was the one to break it. "There's a party tonight," he said. "Over at Aunt Bridget's place. She's going to make a cake with coconut icing."

"That was supposed to be a surprise, young man," Christy said. She was smiling, but there was something uneasy in her bearing, too. She gave Megan a nervous, sidelong glance, so quickly gone that it might have been imaginary.

Aunt Bridget? Megan thought, a beat behind. While Bridget and Christy had made their peace sometime back, they had never been particularly close, even after they buried the proverbial hatchet. They were too different from each other and, at the same time, too much alike, these two cousins.

Later, when she and her sister were working side by side in the corn patch, Megan wielding a hoe and Christy inspecting the stalks and ears for insects, dropping those she found into a can of kerosene, Christy brought up the matter of the party.

"They'll have invited Webb Stratton," she said with a sort of breezy caution. "Bridget and Trace, I mean. They make a point of being neighborly." In truth, most everyone did, for the West could be a hard and empty place, and much was made of even the simplest event.

Megan offered no comment. The summer sun felt good on her back and in her hair; even the ache in her muscles and the new calluses from the handle of the hoe were welcome.

Christy stopped, there in the corn patch, and sought out her children with her eyes. Seeing them tugging up weeds and the occasional sprout with gleeful diligence, a watchful Caney close at hand, she smiled. When she looked at Megan again, though, her gaze was somber. "There's something I need to tell you," she said.

"I suspected that," Megan heard herself say, realizing only as she spoke that she *had* sensed an undercurrent, almost from the moment of her return to her sister's home. She paused and leaned on the hoe handle, gripping it with both hands. "What is it, Christy?"

"You took off so fast, and we'd just reasoned it through—"

Megan waited, braced. Was Christy or Zachary or either of the children sick—even dying? Or was it Caney?

"Bridget and Skye thought we ought to talk about this tomorrow, just the four of us—that's why they haven't been to see you just yet—but I, well, I believe we've let it go too long as it is."

"What are you trying to say?" Megan was becoming frightened by then.

Tears welled in Christy's eyes, but, at the same time, she was smiling. It reminded Megan of spring rain showers sparkling in shafts of sunlight, Christy's smile. "Granddaddy misled us, Megan. They all did. We—you and I and Bridget and Skye—"

Megan closed her eyes, let the hoe fall, forgotten, to the ground. She felt too dizzy to retrieve it. *Don't say it,* she thought. *Don't say we're not really McQuarrys, because I couldn't bear that.*

"We're sisters. The four of us."

Megan stared at her sister, her eyes so wide they hurt. She was at once stunned and relieved. *"What?"*

"We had the same father," Christy said, her voice very quiet. "Different mothers, it would seem, but definitely the same father."

Megan couldn't grasp it. "Papa? Uncle J.R.?"

Christy shook her head. "There was another brother—Thayer. He was Granddaddy's, by a mistress."

Megan remembered her grandfather's passionate

devotion to their beautiful grandmother, Rebecca. "Granddaddy had a *mistress?*"

"It was before he met Grandmother," Christy said gently. "I don't know why they never married. The point is, Thayer was a pure disgrace, and Granddaddy sent him away forever when he was twenty-two, after some dreadful occurrence involving whiskey and a duel. He said Thayer's name was never to be mentioned under his roof again, and, evidently, he meant precisely that."

Megan turned away, started down the row toward the edge of the garden, turned back. Anger was rising inside her, along with confusion and just plain fear. All these years, she'd thought she was one person, and the whole time she'd been another. She was a stranger to herself.

"Don't run away from this, Megan," Christy said, and this time she was all big sister, strong and stubborn. "Thayer McQuarry was our father, yours, mine, Bridget's, and Skye's. Granddaddy didn't want anything to do with him, but he couldn't and wouldn't turn his back on us, so he sent for us, brought us home to be raised by the sons he was willing to claim."

Megan felt sick, then jubilant, then sick again. She pressed the back of one hand to her forehead, let it fall to her side. "Dear God," she whispered.

Christy had put aside the can of kerosene; she came to Megan, sidestepping the fallen hoe, and laid a hand on her shoulder. "It isn't so terrible—is it?"

"Our mothers—?"

"I don't know anything about them," Christy admitted. "Just that they were women Thayer took up with after he left home."

"How—how did you learn—?"

Christy sighed. "When Bridget had the twins, I recorded the births in the McQuarry Bible. That was when I noticed Thayer's name and saw that all four of us were listed as his daughters, not Papa's or Uncle J.R.'s. I guess fooling us was one thing, in Granddaddy's mind, and writing a bald-faced lie in the Good Book was another."

"I was here when little Gideon and Rebecca were born," Megan recalled, and the realization stung. "You knew. You *knew*, Christy McQuarry, and *you didn't tell me!*"

Christy's gaze remained steady, though there was pain in it. Pain and honest regret. "Bridget and I talked the matter out. We decided we'd tell you and Skye when you were older. More settled. Then there was the fire, and after that, you ran away."

"You had no right to keep something like this from me!" Megan accused, stricken. She felt like the lost and wandering ghost of a person who had never truly existed in the first place. "You had no right!"

"I had no choice," Christy corrected. "You ran away!"

Megan clenched her fists at her sides. She'd never struck another human being, and she wasn't about to begin then, but that didn't mean the temptation wasn't there, for it was. God help her, *it was*. "You had plenty of time!"

"But not plenty of information. Eventually, Bridget found a letter from Granddaddy tucked into the lining of the Bible's back cover. After that, we sat Caney down and pried what we could out of her. She still hasn't told all she knows, not by any means."

Megan dashed at her cheeks with the heels of her palms. "She kept the secret? All that time?"

Christy sighed. "She believed she was doing the right thing. Our father was every kind of rascal, Megan. He eventually got himself killed, down in New Orleans. He was—he was caught with another man's wife. Caney thought we had enough grief, the four of us, without that stirred into the pot."

Megan was silent for a long time, trying desperately to regain her equilibrium, both physically and emotionally. When she spoke again, her voice was a raw whisper. "And Skye? How long has she known?"

Christy averted her eyes, but only for a moment. "Since I had Joseph," she answered. "She and Jake were married about that time. And you took off soon after that."

Megan swallowed. She'd been so anxious to rejoin her family, but now she realized shakily, what she really needed was some time apart, a chance to work things through in her mind and heart. She stared at her sister, still astounded, trying to take it all in.

Christy spoke quickly, if calmly. "This is a shock, I know," she said. "But Bridget and Skye and I have all been much closer since we learned the truth."

"You didn't feel—angry?"

"With Granddaddy?" Christy asked, folding her arms as though she'd taken a chill. "Yes, at first. But after a while, I began to understand. He thought he was doing the right thing—the best thing. He loved us, Megan. Enough to bring us home to Virginia, to be brought up as McQuarrys. A lot of people would have turned their backs, pretended we didn't exist. That would have been a lot easier on him and just about everyone else in the family, don't you think?"

Megan's throat thickened to the point where she could barely breathe, but she nodded. She understood—she truly did—but she was a long way from assimilating what she'd learned. When she'd recovered enough to move, she turned, went back to retrieve the hoe she'd dropped, and began hacking methodically at the dirt.

Christy left her to the solace of her work.

Twilight was spilling across the hillsides in purple and blue shadows when Webb rode up to the Qualtrough house. The windows gleamed with welcoming lamplight, and, through the trees on the other side of the creek, he caught the glow of the Shaw place as well. He couldn't help thinking of the darkened, empty rooms he'd left behind half an hour before.

Trace came through the open front door, grinning in the fading daylight. "Where's that yellow dog of yours?" he asked.

"I didn't reckon Augustus was invited," Webb answered.

"Well," Trace allowed, "the least you can do is take him some leftovers."

Webb dismounted, started toward the barn, leading his horse. Trace fell in beside him.

"Mighty glad you could make it," he said.

Webb kept a straight face. "I'm not going to change my mind about selling the land," he said. "You know that, don't you?"

Trace chuckled. "Hell, yes," he said as they reached the corral gate. He worked the latch and swung it open to admit Webb and the gelding. "What I'm wondering is, do *you* know that saying no to a McQuarry woman is just the beginning of a discussion, not the end?"

Webb grinned as he led the horse through, lifted one of the stirrups, and began loosening the cinch to remove the saddle. "I reckon I had an inkling," he replied.

Trace took the saddle, hoisted it easily onto the top rail of the fence, while Webb slid the bridle off and hung it alongside the other tack. "Megan's a fine-looking woman," he said, stepping through the gate again, fastening it when Webb was beside him.

It was all Webb could do not to roll his eyes. "Yes," he agreed, and his voice came out sounding unaccountably gruff. "She surely is."

"You must be mighty lonely, living on that big place all by yourself."

"No more than the next man," Webb answered. Which, he reasoned, was pretty damn lonely, when you thought of all the poor old cowpokes, miners, and timbermen who were living by themselves up and down the banks of Primrose Creek.

Trace thrust a hand through his hair and heaved a heavy sigh. He was a straightforward man, uncomfortable with any sort of deception, however innocent or obvious. "You could use a wife, couldn't you?" he blurted out.

Webb laughed, stopped to face his friend there in the moonlit dooryard of a happy home. "I don't know as *use* is the word I'd employ," he said. "But yes, I wouldn't mind marrying. I'm just waiting for the right woman, that's all."

"Well," Trace replied, exasperated, "maybe Megan is the right woman."

Webb considered the spellbinding red-haired creature waiting inside, with her equally lovely sister and cousins. It was no secret that Trace, Zachary, and Jake were all happy with the marriages they'd made. It was also no secret that the McQuarry females, beautiful as they were, were spirited, mule-stubborn, and overflowing with opinions that didn't necessarily match those of their mates. Such qualities were trying enough in a horse—in a woman, they could cause all manner of sorrow and travail. He had enough to do, starting a ranch, keeping it going, without that.

Didn't he?

"When did you take up matchmaking?" he asked.

He could see Trace redden up, even in the twilight. "It just makes sense, that's all. You need a wife, and Megan needs a husband."

Webb narrowed his eyes, lowered his voice. "What do you mean, 'Megan needs a husband'?"

Trace rasped out a sigh. "Not *that*," he said, and Webb knew if they hadn't been such good friends, Trace probably would have punched him one, right then and there, just for daring to *suggest* that Megan, an unmarried woman, might be in a family way. "She does have, well, a certain reputation around here."

"Ah," Webb said, and folded his arms. The sounds of laughter and clattering pots and dishes came out through the doorway, pulling at him, drawing him in. He stood his ground.

"She ran away and became an actress."

Webb almost laughed out loud. "*God*, no," he mocked. "Not that."

Trace smiled. "Well, it sure riled the ladies of Primrose Creek," he muttered, and Webb knew he wasn't referring to Bridget, Christy, and Skye. With nothing more said, the two men went into the house.

Megan seemed subdued, if not downright retiring, that evening, seated across the Qualtroughs' long trestle table from Webb; he caught her watching him twice, there in the midst of love and noise and children, and each time she flushed and looked away. Webb reminded himself that a shy McQuarry had probably never drawn breath and wondered if it wasn't embarrassment, heightening that rose-petals-and-cream coloring of hers. No doubt she knew her family had hopes of swapping her for six hundred and twenty-five acres of prime land, and, whether she was a party to the plan or not, the whole thing had to be a strain on her pride.

Thanks to his mean, sorry bastard of a father, Thomas Stratton, Sr., not to mention his elder brother, Tom Jr., Webb had long since learned not to let much of anything show in his face or bearing, and the skill stood him in good stead there among all those McQuarrys, Qualtroughs, Shaws and Vigils. Nobody needed to know that he was beginning to find the idea of marriage to Megan McQuarry intriguing, and this after all these years of thinking nobody but Eleanor could rope him in and pasture him out.

He was stirring his after-supper coffee when he felt Megan's gaze touch on him for the third time—it was like a sudden spill of sunshine, though he was sure she hadn't meant to favor him with any sort of warmth or brightness—and looked up idly to meet her eyes. She was glaring at him fit to singe his hide, and that made him grin.

She looked away quickly, and he chuckled under his breath.

"You going to be hiring for spring roundup?" The question came from the other end of the table, and a few ticks of the mantel clock sounded before Webb caught hold of the fact that it was his to answer.

He turned and saw Trace watching him, a biscuit in one hand and a butter knife in the other. "Yep," he answered, more conscious, rather than less, of Megan's presence and her regard. "I need a dozen men, at least. God knows where I'm going to find them, though."

Trace and Zachary made sympathetic noises, while Jake Vigil, the most recent addition to the family, having wed Skye McQuarry a couple of years back, looked downright grim. He ran a big timber outfit, as well as a lumber mill in town, and he and Skye had built a good-sized house on her section of land just down the creek. "Good luck," he said. "Whatever help I've been able to get, I've had to scrape up off the floors of saloons."

Skye, a brown-haired, brown-eyed beauty with a generous mouth and a quietly vibrant nature, was watching her husband with an expression of warm admiration. They had two children in their household, Webb knew: Jake's son, Hank, born of some previous alliance, and a plump baby girl of their own, blessed with her mother's good looks.

Zachary leaned forward in his chair, and, though he

wasn't wearing his badge, the nickel-silver glint of it was always in his eyes. He was quick with that .45 of his, the marshal was, and even quicker with his mind. "There's been a lot of rustling and just general thieving down in the low country," he said, addressing everyone. "Bound to move up this way eventually."

Vigil uttered a sigh of resigned agreement, and Trace nodded glumly. His gaze found Webb and leveled on him. "You might want to start carrying an iron," he said. "Running that place all by yourself the way you do, you'd be easy pickin's."

Megan looked at Webb in alarm, and that cheered him. In spite of herself, she was concerned for his safety. How-do and hallelujah.

He shook his head. He hadn't carried a gun since— well, since the day he'd learned, to his horror, that he was capable of killing a man in cold blood—and he didn't mean to start now. He had a rifle at the ranch, used for hunting and putting down the occasional sick cow or injured horse, but that was all. "No need," he said, his mind swamped, all of a sudden, with stomach-turning images of his elder brother lying broken and bleeding on the ground. Webb had thought Tom was dead, thought he'd done murder, and it still scared him to think how close he'd come to committing the ultimate sin.

"No need?" Megan echoed, speaking directly to Webb for the first time since the evening began. "There are outlaws and renegade Indians in these foothills, Mr. Stratton. There are bears and wildcats and snakes."

He took a sip of his coffee, paused to relish the taste.

While his own brew might have served to strip white-wash off an old outhouse, Bridget's was delicious. "I confess to a fear of wildcats," he said mildly. "Outlaws, Indians, bears, and snakes don't scare me much, though."

Megan narrowed those changeable eyes of hers—now a tempestuous shade of sea-green—and to Webb it seemed that everyone else in that crowded, jovial room receded into two dimensions just then, no more real than figures in paintings, leaving only him and Megan fully present. "Then you're a fool," she said, and her cheeks were mottled with apricot, which meant she hadn't missed his reference to wildcats.

He smiled. "That may be so," he allowed. "Still, I'll leave the gun-toting to your brother-in-law, the marshal here, and handle things my own way."

"I'd be curious to know," she pressed, clearly irritated, perhaps thinking he was overconfident or even arrogant, "how you intend to 'handle'—say—a wildcat?"

A shrill jubilation welled up in his heart, pressed sweetly and painfully against the hollow of his throat, but he let none of what he felt show in his face. "Well, now," he said, "I guess that depends on the wildcat."

Somebody cleared their throat, and suddenly the room was full again, alive again, virtually throbbing with energy, personality, and life. Megan continued to stare at Webb for a few moments, then made a point of looking away.

Confound it, Webb thought. He didn't want to care. He couldn't *afford* to care, not about Megan McQuarry, anyhow. Much as he wanted a wife, she was an unsuitable candidate. Nonetheless, she stuck in his mind like a burr tangled in a horse's tail, and it didn't do any good at all telling himself she was an actress, an independent sort, bound to light out for parts unknown as soon as she got bored. He still couldn't run her out of his head.

Chapter

3

"**W**ell," Bridget demanded, industriously drying dishes as Megan handed them to her, one by one, "what do you think of Webb?"

Skye and Christy were nearby, Skye rocking her daughter next to the fire, Christy clearing the long table. Caney, normally a part of all their get-togethers, was in town, making supper for her beau, Mr. Hicks. The men, mercifully, had gone outside to smoke pipes and cheroots, and the other children were either asleep or chasing each other in the dooryard.

Megan took them in, one by one. Bridget, Christy, Skye. Her *sisters*. She loved them all, and desperately, but she was furious with them, too. They might as well have abandoned her in some cold and desolate place, leaving her in the dark the way they had. "What am I *supposed* to think?" she asked, as the lid began to rattle atop her temper. "That he'd make a good husband?"

They blushed, all three of them, but Megan's mind had long since moved on to another, more pressing subject. "Christy told me," she said very quietly, fixing Skye with a brief, pointed glance. "About Thayer McQuarry and his many exploits."

Bridget's smile was soft and a little rueful. "I only know of four," she commented. "Exploits, I mean. Us."

Nobody commented. At least, not on Bridget's pitiable attempt to lighten the moment.

"How could you?" Megan demanded in a sputtering whisper, and she knew that her eyes were flashing with fury and hurt. "How *could* you, any of you?"

"You didn't give us much of a chance to explain," Bridget observed, setting a clean, dry plate on the shelf next to the stove. Of the four of them, she was always the quickest to find her footing again when she missed a step, which wasn't often. "Running off the way you did, I mean."

Skye's brown eyes were round. "What does it matter now?" she wanted to know, and her tone was mildly plaintive. Family was what counted with Skye; as far as she was concerned, blood truly was thicker than water. "We're all together again. We're *sisters*. What else matters?"

"The *truth* matters," Megan said in an outraged whisper, resting her hands on her hips, the dishtowel dangling like a flag along one thigh. "*Loyalty* matters."

"You're a fine one to talk about loyalty," Bridget remarked calmly. It was hard to nettle her, but once she got her bustle in a tangle, reasonable folks took cover. "Running off like that. Leaving us all to wonder and worry."

Megan slanted a sidelong look at Skye. "Not all," she said, and took no satisfaction in the way her cousin—*sister*—squirmed.

"You made me swear not to tell anyone where you were!" Skye blurted, and her small daughter fidgeted a little, there in her mother's arms, then nestled close and went to sleep. "I should never have promised—"

Bridget and Christy exchanged looks but offered no comment.

Megan wrapped her arms tightly around herself, held on. It was a habit she'd developed as a child, one meant to anchor her emotions, keep her from being carried away by their intensity. Rationally, she understood the situation well enough, but her heart and spirit were still assimilating the reality that she was not the person she'd always believed herself to be. Indeed, her whole sense of identity had been undermined. Perhaps her sisters were content, knowing so little about their common past, but Megan was full of questions, dizzy with them.

One by one, she considered these three beloved strangers who were the heart and life's blood of her family. Bridget had Trace and their flock of children; Christy had Zachary, Joseph, and little Margaret; and Skye had Jake, her stepson Henry, usually called Hank, and baby Susannah. No doubt the hectic pace of their daily lives left them little time to wonder about their disinherited father, their separate mothers, and this final loss of the parents they'd believed to be their own, faults notwithstanding, all these years.

"The letter," Megan managed at last. "Let me see Granddaddy's letter."

Bridget nodded, fetched the McQuarry Bible down from its place of honor on the mantelpiece, and carried it over to the table. Megan sat down, weak in the knees, and stared at the giant black book as though it might contain still more shattering secrets.

It was battered and peeling, and the gold lettering impressed into the cracked leather had worn almost completely away. The corners were curled, the spine was coming loose from the binding, and the pages were translucent with age. Gently, leaning over Megan's shoulder to reach, Bridget turned the Bible facedown and raised the back cover. A vellum envelope protruded from a tear in the ancient lining.

Megan's hand trembled as she removed the missive carefully, opened it, and took out a single sheet of paper.

The handwriting, though faded, was strong, clear, and slanted just slightly to the right, and it was Gideon McQuarry's, without question. Just seeing the familiar shapes of the letters and words made her miss her grandfather with ferocious force, but she was angry, too. Oh, yes, she was angry, and her eyes were so full of tears that she couldn't see to read.

Christy took the letter, sat down beside her with a sigh. "April 17, 1862," she began in a quiet voice. "McQuarry Farm, Virginia.

"My beloved granddaughters,

"Every man must confess his sins, if he is to have any hope of heaven, and deception is certainly a grievous sin. I have deceived you, as have my sons, Eli and J.R., and their wives—they are weak people, all of them, and I dare not depend upon them to make things right when I die. For that reason, I am writing this letter, in the earnest expectation that you will find it one day and learn the truth, however belatedly. It is my prayer that you will come to forgive me in time—"

The letter went on to describe Thayer McQuarry's birth, to an unnamed young woman of Granddaddy's acquaintance. When he married Rebecca, shortly after discovering that he was already the father of a son, Gideon had arranged to raise the boy himself. His son's mother had been relieved, and Rebecca had welcomed the child as her own.

Throughout his life, Granddaddy wrote, Thayer had been a trial, and by the time he reached manhood, he was a blight on the family honor, a blasphemer, drinking to excess, gambling and fighting with his fists, dallying with other men's wives. Granddaddy had finally paid him to leave the farm, and Virginia, forever, and, as Christy had told Megan the day before, he had forbade the remaining members of the family even to speak the man's name in his hearing. Apparently, his instructions had been well heeded, for none of the sisters had ever dreamed their grandfather had sired three sons instead of two.

Thayer had fathered four children after his banishment, and after each birth Granddaddy had sent Caney to fetch the infants home to the farm. As the wives of both his remaining sons had failed to conceive, he had given two babies to Eli and two to J.R., to raise as their own. He'd thought it might have a settling effect on his boys, giving them some real responsibility, but in the end they hadn't done much better than their elder brother would have.

Megan's throat tightened with a welter of emotions as she listened. Granddaddy might never have known their mothers' names, and if he had, he evidently hadn't recorded them, nor did he say where they had been born or, for that matter, precisely when. Even her birthday might be merely an invented date, just another lie.

She flipped to the front of the Bible, where the generations of McQuarry "begats" were recorded, and sought her own name, running a fingertip down the yellowed, brittle pages. *Megan Elizabeth McQuarry,* she read, at long last. *Born in the summer of 1850.*

She swallowed and looked up at her sisters' faces. All of them, to their credit, met her gaze steadily. "Surely *someone* can tell us——"

Christy sighed again, slipped an arm around Megan's shoulders. "I believe Caney knows," she said, "but she's already said more than she wanted to."

"I thought she'd be here tonight," Megan said, still dazed.

Bridget bit her lower lip, then nodded. "She's bound and determined to get Mr. Hicks to the altar before the first snow, and she's been spending a lot of time herding the poor man in that direction."

Megan recalled her exchange with Caney that morning in Christy's kitchen and wondered if Mr. Hicks was the real reason her friend had stayed away from the celebration supper. Caney had been furious with Megan for going off without a word of farewell, two years before, and she'd made no secret of the fact. Very likely, she had simply decided there was nothing to celebrate.

"I need to talk to her," Megan said.

"There's plenty of time for that," Skye assured her.

Little Susannah, a sweet, miniature version of her mother, was sound asleep in her arms by then; she carefully rose from the rocking chair, laid the child on Bridget's horsehair settee, and covered her with a crocheted blanket. "Besides, we've all tried."

"Why wouldn't she tell us everything?" Christy ruminated, frowning. "Caney, I mean."

Bridget was at the stove, pouring hot water from a kettle into a blue china teapot. "It's possible, isn't it, that she truly doesn't know anything more?" she said.

Christy and Skye looked as skeptical as Megan felt. "She knows," they said in concert.

Bridget chuckled ruefully. "I'm sure you're right," she admitted. "I suppose there's some terrible scandal involved."

"How could it be any worse?" Megan demanded.

Bridget rolled her eyes at this, but Christy reached over, took Megan's hand, and squeezed it reassuringly.

"They could have been married to other men—our mothers, I mean," Bridget said. "Or perhaps they were women of ill repute."

Skye paled a little and glanced nervously toward her sleeping child, as though Susannah might have overheard and been scarred by the stigma. "Bridget!" she hissed.

Bridget smiled. She enjoyed stirring embers into flame, always had. "Well, it's possible, isn't it?" she whispered. "It doesn't sound as if our dear old daddy was the sort decent women want to consort with, does it?"

"Nonsense," Christy put in crisply. Both Megan and Skye were somewhat in awe of Bridget, she being the eldest of the four and the most direct in speech and manner, but Christy suffered no such malady. "Men like Thayer McQuarry are *precisely* the sort decent women want to consort with. All we can really conclude concerning our mothers is that they probably weren't overly intelligent."

A silence fell while everyone absorbed the implications of this possibility, and, one by one, they dismissed it with firm shakes of the head. Stupidity was as unacceptable a quality in one's mother as a lack of moral character.

"What does any of this matter?" Skye asked. "It's all behind us. Can't we just move on from here?" Her gaze found Megan, lingered. "Maybe you're not happy to find out that Bridget and I are your sisters, not your cousins, but I think it's some of the best news I've ever heard!"

Megan's heart softened, at least toward Skye. The two of them had been close since babyhood; they'd shared cradles and prams, dolls and ponies, sorrows and secrets. She rubbed her temples with the tips of her fingers. "It's not that simple—at least, not for me."

Skye's expression was typically ingenuous. "Why ever not?" she asked.

"Why indeed?" Bridget pressed, one eyebrow raised.

Megan sat with both hands splayed atop the battered Bible, as though she might divine something more of the mystery that way. "Don't you see?" she whispered, addressing all her sisters without raising her eyes to their faces. "We know nothing at all about our mothers and *next* to nothing about our father. That means we're virtual strangers not only to each other but to ourselves."

Skye knitted her brow, and Bridget checked the pins holding her masses of blond hair in a loose bun at her nape. Christy interlocked her fingers with Megan's. "We're still the same people we've always been, Megan."

Megan nodded, but she was still troubled, still at sixes and sevens. In time, she supposed she would recover—and that was the main difference, she decided, between herself and her sisters. They had had some time to get used to an idea that was utterly new to her.

"I'm going to take some air," she said. Rising somewhat unsteadily from her seat at the table, she made for the door, and no one tried to stop her.

The breeze was cool and fresh, and it braced Megan a little, as always, cleared her head. Stars draped the sky in a silvery net, as if flung there by some celestial fisherman, and crickets took up their distinct chorus in the deep grass. The older children were throwing stones into the creek, while the men stood nearby, their voices riding deep and quiet on the clean night air.

Megan traveled in the other direction, following the moon-washed creek upstream, trying to make sense of things, sort through what she'd learned, decide where she was headed. She'd planned to stay at Primrose Creek, but now she had her doubts about the idea. It was difficult, if not impossible, for a woman to find honest work, especially in such a small community, and she wasn't at all sure she could face a lifetime under someone else's roof, even when that someone else was Christy.

She sniffled, touched the back of one hand to her cheek. The stream whispered and burbled as it danced over the colorful stones worn smooth by years, perhaps even centuries, of its passing.

"I don't reckon you can cook the way your cousin does. Can you?" The voice was Webb Stratton's; she knew that without turning around. While her first impulse was to tell him to go away, in no uncertain terms, she ignored it, because another, greater part of her was so glad of his company.

She turned, arms folded, chin high. Her face was in shadow, and she was fairly certain he wouldn't be able to make out any trace of tears lingering on her face. *Bridget is my sister,* she wanted to say, but she didn't. The knowledge was still too fresh, too raw to share. "Yes, I can cook as well as any woman in the family. Caney taught us all—save Christy, who hasn't the proper bent for it—and she's the very best there is."

Webb stood a few feet away, easy in his skin, sure of his path through a treacherous and confusing world. Megan had once felt that way, but she'd since learned that she'd been wrong to trust her own judgment. She was as lost as any other wandering soul. "I guess I didn't figure an actress would be inclined toward domestic life," Webb ventured.

She stiffened a little, already on the defensive, even though she hadn't perceived a threat. What was it about this man that made her feel like some many-legged creature trying to dance on ice? "I'm a complex person, Mr. Stratton," she said, at some length. "Full of surprises."

"I believe you are," he agreed. "Something's been troubling you tonight. What is it?"

It was a bold question, to say nothing of a blunt one, and to her chagrin she'd answered it before she thought better of the idea. "I'm wondering if I should have come back here," she confided in low tones. "I had a place in this family once, but now I feel as though it might have closed while I was away. Maybe I don't belong here anymore."

Webb was quiet for a long time, and when he spoke, his voice was solemn. "Could be you just need a little distance."

She nodded, though her heart was already breaking at the mere thought of leaving Primrose Creek and the people she loved.

That was when Webb took her by surprise. "I could use a woman over at my place," he said quietly.

Megan was too startled to speak. Surely he hadn't said what she thought he had—had he? What sort of person did he think she was?

He laughed, thrust a hand through his sandy hair. "I didn't mean that quite the way it rolled over my tongue," he said. "Not that you aren't real attractive that way."

Megan opened her mouth, closed it again. She wasn't sure whether she should slap Mr. Stratton across the face and walk away or stay and hear him out. Being even this close to him produced a deliciously disturbing sensation, like falling, deep in her middle, made her want to catch hold of something—

or someone—with both hands. Since he was the only one there, she kept her arms locked around her middle instead.

"What I'm getting at," he went on doggedly, "is that I'd like to hire somebody. To cook and look after the house and all like that. I mean to sign on as many men as I can, like I said at supper, so there'll be a lot of plates to fill."

Megan's lips felt dry; she moistened them with the tip of her tongue. "Are you asking me to come to work as your housekeeper, Mr. Stratton?"

"Webb," he said. "And yes, that's pretty much what I had in mind."

She absorbed that for a moment. "Surely you realize that such an arrangement would arouse gossip."

"I suppose it would," he agreed evenly. "On the other hand, a job is a job. I'll pay you a good salary, and you'll have the whole downstairs to yourself." He paused. "Besides, I don't figure you for the type to turn tail and run because of a few old biddies flapping their tongues."

She'd been right, Megan thought. He was utterly sure of himself. He spoke as though she'd already agreed to go home with him, keep his house, cook his meals. What would it be like, she asked herself, sleeping under the same roof as this man, in a home built on land that had been hers? Would *still* be hers, if she hadn't been so stupid?

"How do I know you'll be a gentleman?" she inquired, mostly stalling. Webb Stratton was probably many things, but he was no fool. He had to know that if he ever forced his attentions upon her, Trace,

Zachary, and Jake would hunt him down and kill him like an egg-sucking dog.

He was holding his hat, and he turned the brim slowly in both hands. His grin flashed white in the darkness. "I'm no gentleman, ma'am," he said, "but that needn't concern you. I'll confine my socializing to town."

Megan was not particularly reassured, for, in point of fact, his kindness made her feel vulnerable rather than safe. Besides, she hated the idea of his "socializing" in town.

"I will not tolerate any sort of foolishness," she warned, just in case he expected more than housekeeping.

He had been about to walk away, back toward the house, probably, to offer his thanks and say his good-byes, but he went completely still when Megan spoke. "You mean you'll take the job?" He sounded pleasantly surprised, as if he'd already resigned himself to being turned down.

"I need work," she said, "and yours is the only respectable opportunity likely to come my way."

He gave a low whistle of exclamation.

"Did you expect me to refuse your offer, Mr. Stratton?"

"Maybe," he said. "Maybe I did, deep down. Fact is, I wasn't entirely sure you wouldn't try to throw me in the creek." He glanced downstream, toward the sound of male laughter and the determined frolicking of tired children, bent on holding off sleep for as long as possible. "I promise you, Miss McQuarry—you won't be sorry you signed on with me. The work will be hard sometimes, when there are a lot of hungry cowboys looking for grub, but no harm will find you on my ranch."

She put out a hand. "Then I accept," she said.

He hesitated, took her hand in his, and shook it. A sweet jolt went through her at his touch. He was strong, his flesh callused by hard work, and yet there was a gentleness in the way his fingers closed around hers that did indeed make her feel looked after, even cherished. "I'll come for you tomorrow," he said. "You're still staying over at Zachary and Christy's place?"

She inclined her head in assent, wondering what her relations would say when she told them she was going to live with Webb Stratton as his housekeeper. No doubt they'd be pleased, not only to have her off their hands but because they'd think their plan was working, that she was going to marry the rancher and bring the lost six hundred and twenty-five acres back into the family circle once and for all.

"I'll be ready," she said, and when he left her, she sighed and tilted her head back to look up at the broad spill of sky stretching from mountain top to mountain top, speckled with stars.

She didn't rest well that night in her old bed at Christy and Zachary's house, but instead thrashed and fretted, caught in a hot tangle of dreams.

"You don't have to do this, you know," Christy said fitfully the next morning, when Megan announced that Webb would be coming by soon to fetch her. "You're perfectly welcome right here."

Megan, standing at the stove, had already made breakfast for Zachary, just to get into practice. Caney either hadn't come home the night before or was still lolling about in bed. "Christy," Megan said gently, "I might have given up my share of the land, but I've still got the pride Granddaddy left us all. I need to make my own way, and I want time to sort things through."

Christy's delicate complexion was flushed, and her gray eyes held sparks. "I declare, Megan McQuarry, your head is hard as tamarack. You belong with your family."

"I *will* be with my family. Just a few miles away, anyway." She spoke softly, for, although she was exasperated with her sister, she loved her as fiercely as ever.

Christy heaved a shuddery sigh. "There will be talk," she warned. "In town, I mean."

The rattles, creaks, and neighs of a team and wagon sounded outside, and Megan felt a wild quickening, brief but shattering, deep in her pelvis. Webb had arrived to fetch her home. *Home.* But the ranch was his place, not hers, not anymore, and she mustn't let herself forget that.

"I'm sure the gossip has already begun," she said, recalling the two townswomen who had sniffed and pulled aside their skirts when she arrived in Primrose Creek. She heard Webb call out to the horses, heard the squeal of brakes as he set the lever. "I need to do this, Christy. I need to make my own way."

Christy started to speak again, then stopped herself and merely nodded.

Megan hurried over to Zachary's shaving mirror, peered into it, and pinched her cheeks to bring some color into her face. Too late, she realized that Christy was watching her with a curious smile.

Webb knocked politely at the door, even though it was wide open to the spring sunshine and wildflower-scented breeze, and Megan had to struggle to keep herself from hurrying across the room to greet him.

Christy did the honors. "Come in, Webb," Megan heard her sister say warmly. "I suspect Megan has already packed her things."

Megan needn't have pinched her cheeks; she could feel a high blush climbing her neck, headed for her hairline.

Webb stood just over the threshold, hat in hand, a cattleman in stance, substance, and manner. Megan wouldn't have traded his company for that of a dozen San Francisco dandies, decked out in silk shirts and polished boots—not just then, anyhow.

"Mornin'," he said, and he ducked his head a little, actually sounded and looked shy.

Megan wasn't fooled. Mr. Stratton was about as reticent as a coiled rattler, and if she didn't keep an eye on him, she was sure to be bitten. "Good morning," she said, her tone cool and more than slightly remote. "I'm ready. If you wouldn't mind fetching my trunk?"

"Point me to it," he said. Christy might not have been there at all, nor the children. It seemed to Megan that the whole world had shrunk away into a vapor, leaving only the two of them, herself and Webb Stratton, in all creation.

She indicated the doorway of her room with a hand that trembled slightly, and after glancing at Christy in an unspoken bid for permission, he proceeded to collect Megan's things from the private part of the house.

"We'll be here if you need us," Christy told her younger sister. "Zachary and the children and I. Right here."

Megan felt her throat swell with all the things she couldn't say. She nodded instead and embraced Christy, and Christy embraced her in return, holding on tightly and for a long time. The two women parted in embarrassment when they realized, simultaneously, that Webb had returned.

Megan took a last look around the house, as though she were setting out on some long journey and might never see it again, then kissed Christy on the cheek and started for the door. Webb was right behind her, easily carrying the big trunk that held all her earthly and unremarkable belongings.

He lowered the tailgate on his buckboard and placed the trunk on the wagon bed, pushing it forward toward the back of the seat. Megan stood waiting until he came to her side and helped her aboard, smooth as a gentleman escorting a lady home from a cotillion.

She gazed straight ahead as he turned the team toward his own place, afraid to look back at Christy for fear her resolve would weaken. She swallowed hard to keep from turning around in the seat to look back.

It never paid to look back. Hadn't Granddaddy said that, more times than she could count?

Webb seemed to know she didn't want to talk, and he held his peace all the way to his ranch house.

When Megan had last seen her section of the Primrose Creek tract, there had been only grass, trees, meadows, and water, with a frieze of mountains edging the blue ceiling of sky. Now the place boasted a house as fine as Bridget's or Christy's, a two-story log structure with glass windows, four chimneys, and a covered veranda out front. The barn was four times the size of the house, Megan noted, and the corral was spacious, fenced with whitewashed rails. Cattle and horses roamed the nearby pastures, grazing in the sweet grass.

She drew in her breath.

"Like it?" Webb asked. His voice was quiet, but there was a note of pride in it.

She sighed. "It's—very nice."

"You could plant a few flowers. Stitch up some curtains, maybe. If you have time, I mean."

"Yes," Megan agreed. She caught hold of her runaway emotions, gathered up her skirts, and made to climb down from the wagon. Webb caught hold of her arm and held her fast in the seat.

"Sit tight," Webb said. "I'll help you down."

She was unnerved by the idea of his hands on her waist, but she didn't have the strength to resist. "Very well," she murmured, and the next thing she knew, she was suspended between heaven and earth, Webb's strong hands clasping her sides. It seemed that she hung there, a creature of neither ground nor sky, for an eternity, looking down into Webb's eyes.

"I'll show you to your room," he said, walking away, lowering the tailgate with a clatter, dragging the trunk across the wagon bed so he could lift it into his arms. "I reckon you'll want to spend the rest of the day getting settled."

Megan merely nodded, at a loss for words. Then she heard a dog barking exuberantly and turned to see a great yellow hound bounding toward them from the direction of the barn.

"That's just Augustus," Webb said, passing her with the trunk, headed toward the house. "He's given to a variety of enthusiasms, but he won't hurt you."

It had never entered Megan's mind that the animal would do her injury. She loved anything with four feet and fur, and Augustus most certainly fit the bill.

"Hullo," she greeted him.

He jumped up, resting his huge paws on her shoulders, and licked her face.

Megan laughed.

"Augustus," Webb growled, without even looking back. "Get down."

Augustus ignored his master and laved Megan from chin to forehead, all over again, making a jubilant whimpering sound in his throat the whole while.

Megan ruffled him behind the ears, and he dropped to all fours then, panting, to trot along at her side as she followed Webb toward the house.

The inside was cool and clean, smelling of beeswax, lamp oil, and recent wood fires. A hooked rug lay on the floor in front of the kitchen fireplace, and Augustus plopped himself down on it with a long-suffering sigh, as though exhausted.

Megan took in the fine big cookstove, the open shelves lined with canned goods, sundries, and neatly stacked blue dishes, the planed and polished floors. Although there was nothing feminine about the place, it was welcoming, in a rustic sort of way, and Megan began to think in terms of pictures on the walls, potted geraniums, and good things baking in the oven. It wasn't a long leap from there to flocks of fair-haired children, some with their father's periwinkle eyes, some with green.

"You'll be sleeping in here," Webb said, his voice echoing from a room just off the kitchen.

Megan gathered her wits and followed the sound. The room was small, but it had a high window and a little stove for cold high-country nights. The bed was narrow and looked as though it might have been hauled in from the bunkhouse, but there was a nice quilt for a coverlet, and the pillow looked soft.

Under the window was a wash stand, again very plain, topped with a basin and pitcher, white enamel, lined at the rims with red and chipped black here and there. He'd set out a towel and a bar of store-bought soap, and Megan was oddly touched by the sight. Webb had taken pains to see that she felt at home, she could tell that much.

"You can hang your clothes on these pegs," he said, quite unnecessarily, gesturing toward a row of wooden dowels nailed to a long, rough-hewn board and attached to the wall.

"Thank you," Megan said. She was wearing the only presentable dress she possessed, having refused the garments Christy had wanted to give her, unable to bear being the recipient of charity, even from her sister. What would her new employer think when he entered the kitchen one morning soon and found his housekeeper dressed in taffeta and feathers or beaded and ruffled silk? She smiled to think of it.

Webb went to the door, giving her a surprisingly wide

berth as he passed, considering the fact that the room was hardly larger than a fruit crate. "If Augustus decides to come calling," he said, "just show him the way out."

Megan nodded, oddly unable to speak.

She was a wanderer, with no place of her own. So why did she feel, for the first time in her life, as though she'd finally come home?

Chapter

4

∽

*M*egan's first housekeeping task was making breakfast for Webb, since he hadn't eaten, and by the time he came in from the barn, she had biscuits ready, along with thick sausage gravy. She was amused and oddly touched to see that he filled a plate for Augustus and set it on a sunny spot in the middle of the kitchen floor before starting his own meal. Megan had had toasted bread and a poached egg at Christy's, so she wasn't hungry.

She assessed the contents of the shelves while Webb and the dog ate with impressive appetite.

"This is good," Webb said between helpings. He sounded surprised. Again.

Megan allowed herself a brief smile, though she tended to concentrate purely on the business at hand, whatever it might be, and at that moment, she was making a mental grocery list. "Thank you," she said. "I can ride, too, and herd cattle, if you have need of that."

Hadn't he and the other men bemoaned the lack of workers in and around Primrose Creek just the night before?

She heard him lay down his fork. "That's no work for a woman," he said.

Megan's list blew out of her mind like feathers scattering in a brisk wind. She turned. "I beg your pardon?" she said. Augustus whimpered once, as though sensing the approach of something ominous.

Webb's eyes danced; plainly, her annoyance amused him, and that realization added fuel to a kindling fire. "What I meant was, I didn't hire you to ride herd, brand, or check fence lines. There's plenty right here to keep you busy."

Megan frowned. "But if you're short-handed——"

"Short-handed?" Webb echoed. "I'd have to hire three or four men before I could call myself short-handed. I reckon I'm going to have to ride down to Virginia City and see if I can scare up a few cowpunchers." He paused. "Is there any more coffee?"

She fetched the pot from the stovetop, carried it over to the table, and refilled his cup. He and the dog had left their plates clean, and that pleased her. Augustus probably would have eaten anything, it was true, but Webb had enjoyed her cooking, and that gave her the first real sense of accomplishment she'd had in a long time. Still, she was nettled by his assumption that she couldn't manage range work.

"Apparently, you don't understand what it means to be a McQuarry," she said.

Webb nodded toward the chair across the table from his. "Sit down," he told her quietly. Because the words had the tone of an invitation rather than a command, Megan complied.

"What," he asked when she was settled, "does it mean to be a McQuarry?"

She was shaken by the tenderness of the question and by the genuine interest she saw in Webb's eyes. He wasn't just asking to be polite, he truly wanted to know. Or did he? She'd once thought the same thing about Davy, and look where *that* had gotten her. She bit her lower lip, stalling, and then sighed. "I've been able to ride since I could walk, Mr. Stratton. I can shoot, too, and I've rounded up my share of cattle, as it happens."

"Bringing the milk cows in from the pasture isn't what I had in mind," he said. "You won't be called on to do any shooting at all, and if you find yourself with time on your hands, I could use some new shirts. You sew, don't you?"

She nodded. In truth, she'd never done more with a needle and thread than put up a hem or repair a torn seam, but she could do virtually anything she set her mind to, she was certain of that.

"Good," he said. "Maybe you could drive into town later. Pick out some yard goods and the like."

She'd have to face the townspeople eventually anyway, might as well get it over with and let them all know she wouldn't be cowed by their disapproval. "All right," she agreed, and she must have sounded a little uncertain, because she saw something like sympathy in Webb's eyes.

She hated sympathy; it was close kin to pity, and Megan could not tolerate that. Years before, when she and Christy had traveled to England with the woman they'd believed to be their mother, the two of them had been promptly shipped off to St. Martha's, a venerable boarding school chosen by their English stepfather, where they had been viewed as uncouth colonials, hailing from a country where slavery was practiced. They'd been penniless into the bargain and frightfully homesick for Granddaddy and the farm, and those pupils who hadn't scorned them had felt sorry for them. Some did both.

"What's going on in that head of yours?" Webb asked forthrightly.

Once again, Megan felt compelled to raise her guard. She wasn't about to share the memories that still bewildered her at times, still ached in the corners of her spirit like new bruises. She hadn't told Skye about those hurts, or even Christy. "I was thinking that you need flour and sugar, not to mention lard," she lied. "Are there chickens?"

"Chickens?" he echoed, as though he'd never heard of the species.

"You know," she prompted cheerfully, "those creatures with beady eyes and feathers. They lay eggs and make a wonderful Sunday supper, fried and served with mashed potatoes."

Mirth lighted his eyes again. "Oh," he said. "Those. Well, no. I don't guess I've gotten around to that yet."

"We must have chickens," Megan said.

"I'll put up a coop while you're fetching what you need from town," Webb replied. "You don't mind going by yourself, do you?"

She shook her head. She'd made the trip many

times, of course, and she was used to doing things on her own.

Twenty minutes later, Megan was driving toward Primrose Creek in her employer's buckboard, a list in one pocket of her dress and a fair amount of Mr. Stratton's money in the other. It occurred to her that she could just keep going, taking the funds, the team, and the wagon with her, but she never seriously considered the idea. She wasn't a thief, and she wasn't going to run away if she could help it. She'd made up her mind, during the long night just past, to set her heels, dig in, and stay put.

Some of her resolve evaporated, however, when she drew stares just by driving down the main street of town. Determined, she stopped the wagon in front of old Gus's general store and secured the team, watching out of the corner of her eye as a gaggle of women clad in calico and bombazine collected on the board sidewalk out front. She heard the whispers, and color flared in her face, but she managed a polite smile all the same. She had been an actress, after all, and a good one.

"Your eyes do not deceive you, ladies," she said, spreading her arms and executing a very grand curtsey. "Megan McQuarry has returned to Primrose Creek in all her glory."

The women muttered and looked to each other for assurance that, yes, they'd really seen this brazen creature, really heard her *dare* to speak to them in such an impudent fashion.

"Humph," said a plump, white-haired woman, barely taller than the metal jockeys that had served as hitching posts in front of the old McQuarry farmhouse. In her rustling black dress, she resembled a squat crow.

When a feminine laugh came from somewhere nearby, Megan and all the ladies turned their heads to see Diamond Lil herself looking on, from just a little way down the sidewalk. She was a splendid creature, Lil was, tall and slender, with deep black hair and amber eyes. She wore the latest San Francisco fashion in pink and gold silk, and her lacy parasol was a work of art, all on its own.

"Don't mind the welcoming committee," Lil said to Megan, as though the half-dozen townswomen were no more cognizant of her words than the street itself or the display of work boots in the window of Gus's store. "They've got nothing better to do with their time, I reckon, than to keep track of your comings and goings."

Megan stared at Lil, fascinated. She'd never seen the woman up close, though she was an institution in Primrose Creek, owning several businesses besides her infamous saloon. Then she put out a hand. "Megan McQuarry," she said.

Lil took the offered hand, shook it graciously. "Lillian Colefield," she replied. "Well, now," she said, looking Megan over. "I heard tell you were an actress."

Gasps and mutters arose from the cluster of Primrose Creek's version of high society.

Megan swept them all up in a quelling glare before meeting Lil's steady gaze again. "Yes," she said clearly.

"I've been thinking of opening a show house, next to my saloon. I might be looking to hire somebody like you."

The ladies clucked at this, like scalded hens, and Megan stifled a laugh. She'd taken a job with Webb Stratton, and she had no reason to leave, but it was nice to know she had another option. "Thank you," she said. "I'll keep that in mind."

Lil was studying the wagon and team. "That looks like Webb Stratton's rig," she said.

Megan felt the words like a punch—it was none of her business, what Webb did when he came to town, she reminded herself—but hid her reaction by broadening her smile. "I'm his housekeeper," she said in a voice meant to carry.

More murmurs among the ladies. This was turning out to be a fruitful day for them, Megan reckoned.

Lil obviously enjoyed the reactions to Megan's announcement. "Well, now," she said. "Lucky you."

Megan felt her color heighten, though she wasn't precisely sure why that should have happened. It wasn't as if there was anything going on between her and Mr. Stratton, after all. She was merely his housekeeper. "I guess I'd better get my marketing done," she said, "while I've still got work."

"You come see me if you have a mind to perform in my theater," Lil reiterated.

"I will," Megan promised. She had enjoyed acting, if not the attendant way of life, but she hoped she wouldn't end up treading the boards again, out of choice or necessity. She wanted to soak in sunshine, not the faint glow of footlights, and she was all too aware that her sisters would suffer a great deal at the hands of the ladies of Primrose Creek if she took up with the likes of Diamond Lil Colefield. "Thank you," she said once more.

Inside the store, Gus greeted her with a jovial smile. Dear Gus. He hadn't a pretentious bone in his big, bearlike body, and he'd been a good friend to the McQuarrys from the first. She well remembered the day, soon after she and her sister and Caney had arrived at Primrose Creek, that Christy had gone resolutely to town to sell their mother's brooch for desperately needed funds. Gus had given Christy fifty dollars—a fortune—for the pin and held on to it, making it clear that Christy should come back for it when she had the means. Later, when he and Christy were married, Zachary had reclaimed the piece as a gift for his bride.

"Hullo, Gus," she said warmly.

"Miss Megan," he boomed, plainly delighted. "Welcome, welcome!"

She smiled as she brought the shopping list out of her pocket. "I've come for supplies," she said. Soon, she was happily examining sturdy cotton cloth for the shirts Webb wanted, while Gus gathered the items scribbled onto a piece of brown wrapping paper and placed them carefully in wooden crates.

When she'd finished making her selections, and Gus's sister, Bertha, had cut the lengths of fabric Megan had chosen, she paid the bill in full and couldn't help noticing Gus's gratitude and Bertha's frank surprise. Times had been hard around Primrose Creek since the big forest fire two years before, when most of the town had burned, and a lot of people were probably letting their accounts go unpaid.

Gus loaded the crates into the wagon, chattering in his broken English the whole while. He had some chicks ordered from the widow Baker's farm, he said, and promised to bring out a batch as soon as they arrived. Like Lil, he had raised Megan's spirits considerably, making her feel welcome, and she was in a cheerful state of mind as she headed back toward Webb's ranch.

Webb's ranch. Best she remember that.

Reaching the far western side of Bridget and Trace's land, which bordered the acres she'd sold to Stratton, she stopped the team and wagon on a knoll and sat surveying all she had given up. A crushing wave of regret crashed over her, followed by fury, with herself and with Davy Trent. Resolutely, Megan brought down the reins smartly and got the rig moving again, jostling and jolting down the hillside toward the house Webb had built.

He'd been sawing wood in the side yard, apparently for the chicken coop, and he wasn't wearing a shirt. His suspenders dangled at his sides, and he was sweating. Megan willed herself to look away, but she found that she couldn't.

He grinned and shrugged into his shirt, leaving it to gape. His hands rested on his hips. "Looks like you laid in enough grub to last right through till next spring," he observed. He seemed pleased.

"It would be nice to have some beef and a side of pork," she said in a businesslike fashion, feeling her flesh blaze with heat as he lifted her down from the wagon. What in the name of all that was holy was wrong with her, she wondered. Perhaps she was coming down with a fever. "Do you have a springhouse?"

His hands lingered at the sides of her waist for the

merest fraction of a moment, but it was long enough to send fire shooting through Megan's most private regions. "An ice house," he said. "I'll show you, after I unload these crates."

She allowed him to help, not because she was lazy or because the work was too much for her, but because she felt hot and a bit dizzy. Sunstroke, she mused. Red-haired people had to be careful about getting too much sun.

When all the crates were inside, Webb led the way to the ice house. It was a cave, dug into the side of a knoll and lined with straw. Blocks of ice, probably hauled down out of the mountains in the height of winter, cooled the dank air. A deer carcass hung from a hook in one of the beams holding up the sod roof.

"Venison," Megan said, already planning dinner.

"Sounds good," Webb replied. He was standing in the doorway, his arms folded, watching her. Because his face was in shadow, she could not read his expression, but his voice was warm and quiet, establishing an intimacy between them that should have unsettled Megan but didn't. "How did things go in town?"

Megan couldn't resist telling him. Her smile was mischievous, though she figured he wouldn't see it in the gloom. "Diamond Lil offered me a job, acting in her new show house. I guess you'd better be nice to me—it seems I'm quite sought after."

He laughed, one shoulder braced against the heavy framework of the door. "I'll keep that in mind," he said.

Megan was conscious of the things inside the house, needing to be put in their proper places, but Webb was blocking the way out. Though there was nothing threatening in his manner—indeed, Megan felt drawn to him, not repelled—she didn't dare try to press past him.

"I—I have work to do," she said.

His grin flashed. "Me, too," he agreed. Then, to Megan's enormous relief, he turned and walked away, leaving the passage clear.

Megan dashed out as if the place had caught fire and flames were licking at her heels. Temporarily blinded by the bright sunlight, she crashed right into Webb's back and would have fallen if he hadn't turned around quickly and clasped her upper arms in both hands to steady her. She was as mortified as if she'd deliberately flung herself at him—not that she'd ever do such a thing.

He stared down at her, still holding her. Then he laughed, low in his throat, and let her go. "Watch out," he counseled. "You might just fall."

Indeed, she thought, she might fall. Maybe she already had.

Megan had been keeping house for Webb Stratton for a full three days before Skye and Caney came to pay a social call. They found her in the bunkhouse, sweeping the floor. It was a new building, never used by cowboys, although a few rats and other creatures had obviously made their nests inside. Webb had left for Virginia City that morning, hoping to hire a crew, and Megan had been working hard ever since, mostly to distract herself from the fact that she already missed him.

Not that she had any right or reason to think about

the man, one way or the other. It just seemed that she couldn't help herself.

Augustus, sleeping in a pool of sunlight just inside the bunkhouse door, roused himself to greet the company with friendly, speculative *woofs* and some hand-licking. Skye laughed and ruffled his ears. Caney surveyed the newly washed window, open to the breeze, and the thin mattresses rolled up on the metal cots lining both walls.

"So you ain't forgotten how to work," the older woman observed.

Skye elbowed her. "Stop your fussing," she said, but there was long-standing affection in her tone. "You've no call to be so contrary."

Megan stood still, broom handle in hand, amazed to find herself with guests. "Come into the house," she said. "I'll brew some tea."

"I'd like to see where you sleep," Caney announced.

Megan and Skye exchanged looks, then avoided each other's eyes lest they break into giggles, the way they'd done so often when they were girls.

"I have the whole downstairs to myself," Megan said, leading the way across the yard and in through the kitchen door. Augustus trotted along at her side, his great broom of a tail swaying from side to side.

"I'll have me a look just the same," Caney said.

Megan sighed. Inside the kitchen, she paused to wash her hands and splash her face at the basin. After using the damask towel on the rod above the small table, she showed them her room, with its narrow bed, its window, its row of pegs, where her dresses hung. She had eight, none of them really suited to life on the banks of Primrose Creek, but they were her own, and she took care of them.

Caney inspected everything—the stove, the quilt, the latch on the window. There was a look of solemn concentration on her face.

"Satisfied?" Megan asked, arching an eyebrow.

Caney huffed but said nothing.

"Let's have that tea," Skye suggested, speaking brightly.

Megan smiled and nodded.

Back in the kitchen area, Skye and Caney took seats at the table, while Megan set about brewing tea.

"Where is that man, anyhow?" Caney demanded.

"I assume you mean Mr. Stratton?" Megan inquired. Caney had always been bristly, even at the best of times, and the very fact that she had come to call was reassuring. "He's gone to Virginia City to hire cowhands."

Skye looked worried. "You're staying here all by yourself?"

Megan didn't reply, since the answer was so obvious.

"I declare," marveled Caney.

"Oh, for heaven's sake," Megan snapped, reaching the end of her patience. "I'm a grown woman." Augustus came to her, toenails *click-click*ing on the wood floor, and nuzzled her right hand. "With a dog. Besides, I've been wanting time to think, remember?"

"That hound don't amount to no kind of protection," Caney protested. At least she was speaking to Megan; that was something. "You best come on back over the creek and sleep at Miss Christy's till Webb gets home."

Megan had no intention of leaving the house unattended, even for a night. She had things to do. "I'm making shirts for Mr. Stratton," she said, although she did not call Webb "Mr. Stratton" anymore or even think of him except in terms of his Christian name. "I've made patterns from newspaper and pinned them to the cloth, but I'm afraid to cut out the pieces."

Caney waved a hand. "I'll show you how to do that," she said.

It was tantamount to a hug and kiss, that statement, given the rift that had opened between Caney and the youngest of her four charges. At least, Megan *thought* she was the youngest. Now she wasn't sure of anything, where she and her sisters were concerned.

Megan set water on to heat and measured dried tea leaves into a pot. "Thank you," she said mildly, and turned her attention to Skye. "Where is little Susannah this fine day?"

Skye beamed at the mention of her daughter. "She's with Bridget."

Megan came to the table and sat down while she waited for the kettle to boil. "You're happy with Jake, aren't you?" she asked softly.

"Deliriously," Skye said, and blushed.

Megan turned her gaze to Caney. "What about you? Have you made any progress with Mr. Hicks?"

Caney's expression darkened with the approach of a storm. "Don't you mention that man's name to me. I done showed him the road."

Megan was stunned, while Skye looked distinctly uncomfortable and, at one and the same time, amused.

"What?" Megan asked, certain that she must have heard wrongly.

"I'm done waitin' for that man to marry up with me," Caney went on. Apparently, if she was going to refer to Malcolm Hicks at all, she was going to call him That Man and nothing else. "I told him, 'You go find some other woman to mend your socks and listen to your tall tales and boil up pig's feet and beans for your dinner. I'm through.'"

"But why?" Megan was truly surprised. Caney had always been so resolute, so diligent, in her pursuit of Mr. Hicks's affections. "I thought you loved him."

Caney's beautiful black eyes filled with tears. "I want to be his wife, not his woman. Unless he declares hisself and stands up with me, in front of Reverend Taylor, things ain't never goin' to change."

The kettle began to boil, and Megan got up, crossed to the stove, and, using an empty flour sack for a pot holder, removed it from the heat. When the tea was brewing, she returned to the table. "I'm sorry," she said, and she meant it. "I suppose he'll come around, though. He must miss you terribly."

"Humph," Caney said. "Where's them yard goods you were talking about?"

"I'll get them after we have tea," Megan replied gently.

"Don't want no tea," Caney replied.

Megan fetched the stack of folded fabrics from her room and set them on the kitchen table. Caney immediately spread them out to have a look, while Skye poured tea for herself and Megan. They sipped, keeping their cups at a thoughtful distance from the lengths of cloth their friend was inspecting.

"You measured that man's shoulders?" Caney asked. " 'Fore you made the pattern, I mean?"

Megan nodded. It brought on another rush of inner heat, remembering how she'd used lengths of string to chart the dimensions of Webb's upper body.

"He's a big man," Caney commented.

"Umm-hmm," Megan said, averting her own gaze only to be snagged by Skye's bright, too knowledgeable glance.

"Fine-looking, too," Skye said.

"Is that any way for a married woman to talk?" Megan challenged, but she was smiling. Webb was indeed fine-looking.

"Why do you suppose he don't have himself a wife, a man like that?" Caney speculated. She was apparently satisfied with Megan's sewing project, so far, for she'd helped herself to a pair of scissors and started cutting out a shirtsleeve.

Megan had asked herself the same question, but she'd never asked Webb, and she had no intention of doing so. It wasn't that she didn't want to know if he'd ever loved a woman—she did—but if he told her about his past, she'd have to reciprocate, and she wasn't ready to do that. Not yet.

"Maybe he was waiting to find the right woman," Skye said, her words accompanied by the *snip-snip* of the scissors and Augustus's deep, contented sigh. The dog was lying at Megan's feet, his large, soft body warm against her ankle. "Webb, I mean."

Megan blushed. "Maybe he's already got a wife someplace," she said.

"Nonsense," Skye scoffed. "She'd be here with him if he did."

Megan wasn't sure why she was arguing the point; if

she were perfectly honest, she'd admit that she purely *hated* the thought of Webb being married. Which was completely unreasonable of her, of course, since Mr. Stratton's private life was no concern of hers. She was there to cook, clean, and sew, and that was all.

She sighed. "Maybe," she agreed. Whether Webb had ever taken a wife or not, there were bound to be women in his life. Hadn't he told her, straight out, that he would confine his romantic interests to the ladies who worked for Diamond Lil? It made her blood sting as though it had turned to kerosene, just thinking about what probably went on in places like that.

Caney had finished cutting out the first shirt and advanced to the second, after rearranging some of the pattern pieces to suit her. "One way you could find out, and that's to ask him," she said. "If he's got hisself a wife somewheres, I mean."

Megan was mortified. "I wouldn't!" she gasped, coloring up.

Skye smiled over the rim of her teacup. "But you do want to know—don't you?"

Megan glared at Skye. "No."

"Don't lie to me. I know you too well. You're *smitten.*"

"I am not!"

Caney made a *tsk-tsk* sound with her tongue. "You two. Carryin' on just like you did when you was babies."

Megan and Skye exchanged another glance, but this one was serious.

"How old was I when I came to Granddaddy's farm?" Megan asked quietly.

Caney paused in her snipping and looked at Megan,

and her eyes were dark pools of sadness and inherited suffering. She pressed her full lips together, and for a moment, Megan thought she would refuse to answer. She had been standing to cut out the shirts, but now she sank into her chair, as though too weary to stand. "You, Miss Megan, were about two weeks old."

"Where did I come from?"

Caney was silent for a long time, but her gaze was steady. "I reckon you know you were Mr. Thayer's child, just like the others."

"That isn't what I meant," Megan said.

Caney heaved a sigh. "You were born in New Orleans. Your mama died, having the pair of you."

Both Megan and Skye went so still that they might have been statues in some Greek garden, frozen in moonlight.

"The pair of us?" Skye echoed. She'd set her teacup down, but her hands were still trembling.

Caney's eyes brimmed with fresh tears. "You're twins, the two of you. Oh, you never looked alike, that's true enough, but there's always been a special bond holdin' you together. Didn't you ever wonder about that?"

Instinctively, Skye and Megan linked hands, held on tightly, though all their attention was fixed on Caney.

"Why?" Megan breathed. "Why didn't you *say something*?"

"I promised your granddaddy I wouldn't, that's why," Caney said. "If I could go back, I wouldn't do any different. There's been enough trouble in this family."

Skye was breathing deeply and slowly, as though

trying to keep her composure, and her fingers clung to Megan's. "Tell us," Megan insisted, "what you know about our mother."

"Was she—was she a lady of the—the evening?" Skye dared to ask.

Caney's face was lined with pain and reluctance and the knowledge that it was futile trying to hold the old secrets at bay. "She was an Irish serving girl," she said. Her countenance darkened again. "Sixteen years old. Prettiest thing you ever saw."

"Did our father abandon her?"

"That rascal," Caney said, her tone edged with an old fury. "Never you mind him. Your mama, she died the day after you were born. Wouldn't have been able to keep two little babies anyhow. She had no family, and the people she worked for had already turned her out. She'd have starved to death if Gideon McQuarry hadn't heard about her and stepped in to make sure she had a decent place to stay and food to eat."

Some of the luster had gone off that glittering summer day, for Megan at least, thinking of that poor young girl, destitute except for the kindness of a stranger, but at least she knew where she'd come from. And she was Skye's twin. The knowledge was wondrous, and, at the same time, it seemed as though she'd always known.

"What was her name?" Skye asked.

Caney sighed. "Maureen," she recalled, very softly. "I didn't know her for long. Your granddaddy sent me to look after her, down there in New Orleans. I was supposed to bring her and her baby home to Virginia, once the birth was over—nobody dreamed there was two of you—but the chile was plumb done in. Mr. Thayer, he done broke her, someplace deep inside. She hung on for a day, then she just closed her eyes and died. Saddest thing I ever did see."

Megan and Skye were both silent, envisioning the scene. Skye had borne a child, and Megan could imagine what it must be like. They understood Maureen's ordeal well enough.

"Who was born first?" Megan asked.

"Who named us?" Skye wanted to know, her words tumbling over Megan's, tangling with them.

Caney's smile was sad. "Miss Skye, you were the first one born. Five minutes later," she went on, turning to Megan, "you came along. Your mama gave you your names—she'd been saving them up, I think."

"And our father?"

"Thayer McQuarry?" Caney made another gesture with her hand, one of dismissal, angry and blunt. "That scoundrel? He'd landed himself in jail by that time."

"Jail?" Skye asked.

"He'd got himself into another duel," Caney explained. She rose back to her feet and began to cut fabric again, taking refuge in work as she had always done. "Killed a senator's son. He was hanged a month later."

Megan put a hand to her mouth.

"I wish we'd never asked," Skye murmured, her dark eyes haunted.

Caney's smile was all the more powerful for being totally unexpected. "Well, now," she said, "that's the thing with a McQuarry. They just keep on askin' until they find out the truth, even when it would be better not to know."

Neither Megan nor Skye even tried to deny that. Their granddaddy had taught them most everything they needed to know to get on in life—except when to quit.

Chapter

5

"Webb? That you?"

Webb, bellied up to the bar in Virginia City's infamous Bucket of Blood Saloon, glanced up from the glass of whiskey he had yet to touch and stared in amazement into the greasy, bottle-lined mirror. He turned and faced his younger brother, Jesse. Seven years before, when Webb had seen him last, Jesse had been just sixteen, green and gangly, but he was a man now, pure and simple. There was a stony glint in his blue eyes that troubled Webb, but the .45 riding low on the kid's hip bothered him a lot more.

"What the hell are you doing here?" he asked.

Jesse's Adam's apple bobbed at the base of his throat, went still again. He edged up to the bar and stood shoulder to shoulder with Webb, studying their reflections in the big mirror. Except for the ten years that lay between them—eventful years, into the bargain—they looked much alike. "I might ask you the same question," Jesse responded at last.

"I'm looking to hire some cowpunchers," Webb allowed. "How's Pa?" he asked when Jesse didn't speak again right away. Any mention of his family was deeply personal to Webb; he'd never discussed them with anyone at Primrose Creek, even though he considered that his home. He didn't worry about being overheard, though; the Bucket of Blood was a noisy place, even in the middle of the day, filled with tinny piano music, the click of pool balls, the arguments and celebratory whoops of its most dedicated patrons.

Jesse nodded to the bartender, and a glass was set before him. He poured a helping from Webb's bottle, raised it in a mocking toast, and drank. "Pa? Well, he's meaner than he ever was," he said.

Webb closed his eyes. *Mean* wasn't a fit word to describe the old man; he made a grizzly with a mouthful of wasps seem cordial.

"He never put a bounty on my head?" he asked after a few moments, taking a drink at last. His hand shook a little as he raised the glass, and he hoped his kid brother hadn't noticed.

"Why the devil would he do that?" Jesse asked. "He'd rather shoot you himself."

Webb sighed. "And Eleanor?" he asked very quietly. It was odd; he'd loved Eleanor Stratton, his sister-in-law, from the day she came to the Southern Star as his elder brother's bride, and once she'd turned to him for comfort and given him reason to believe she felt the same way. Now, when he tried to assemble her features in his mind, all he could see was Megan McQuarry's face.

"Same as usual," Jesse allowed. "At least, she was

fine last time I was there. That was a couple of years back. I'm not much more welcome on the old place than you are, big brother."

Webb had expected Eleanor to return to her home folks back east after Tom was killed. After *he* had killed Tom, beat him to death with his bare hands. The memory brought up his gorge, and he pushed the glass away, his mind awash in blood. His brother's blood. "I'm surprised she stayed," he said at some length, and his voice sounded gruff and strange, even in his own ears. "At least I figured she'd remarry and move to town."

Jesse looked puzzled. Time had hardened him, and there was a bleak distance in his eyes that gnawed at Webb in some deep and hurtful place. He'd been all Jesse had, and he'd abandoned him. If the boy had gone wrong in the meantime, Webb would have to claim his share of the fault. "I reckon Tom would frown on that," he said.

For Webb, it seemed that all the mechanisms of heaven and earth, seen and unseen, ground to a halt in that moment. Tom was dead. Webb had knelt beside his body, in the tide of receding rage, and felt for a pulse. There hadn't been one.

Suddenly, Jesse laughed. "Good God," he rasped, refilling his glass nearly to the brim. "You thought you killed him!"

Even in the Bucket of Blood, such a remark was likely to draw attention. Webb grabbed the whiskey bottle with one hand and his younger brother's elbow with the other, then hustled him toward the swinging doors. Outside, on the sloping wooden sidewalk, Jesse still laughed. Webb dragged him into an alley, dropped the bottle to the ground, where it shattered musically, caught Jesse by the lapels of his worn shirt, and hurled him backward against a clapboard wall.

"He's alive?" he demanded. "Tom is *alive?*"

Jesse's face went cold, and he shrugged out of Webb's grip. "Yeah, no thanks to you. Took him a year to get over the thrashing you gave him."

Webb closed his eyes, but the memories pursued him all the same, glaring and fresh, acrid with the stench of blood. He'd found Ellie hiding in the corn patch that morning seven years back, her delicate arms covered with bruises, her eyes blackened. He'd raised her to her feet, led her back to the house, and attended to her wounds as gently as if she were a child. She hadn't admitted, even then, that Tom had come in drunk, sometime in the night, and taken his fists to her, but Webb had known. He hadn't been at home himself the previous evening, or he might have heard her screams. God knew he'd heard them before, and he'd intervened before, too.

"Leave him," he'd said. "I'll look after you."

She'd stared at him, dazed, and shook her head, curled in on herself like a small animal trying to shield itself from further blows. He carried her to his own bedroom, laid her down, and covered her gently. Then, coldly furious, he'd gone in search of Tom.

"They've got a boy now," Jesse said, in a more prudent tone, bringing Webb back from the ugliest regions of his mind. "Named him Tom the third."

Webb wished he hadn't dropped the whiskey, because he sure could have used a drink just then. In point of fact, he could have used a whole still. "How old?" he ground out.

"The boy?" Jesse frowned, but there was something in his eyes, a knowledge, a suspicion. A smirk displaced the frown. "I reckon he'd be about six by now. Ellie must have been carrying him when you gave Tom that licking."

Webb cursed. "Did he—does he—?"

"Does Tom still get drunk and pound on Ellie?" Jesse asked, with no discernible emotion. "No. Once she had the boy, she changed. Wouldn't take no grief from him or anybody else, including Pa. First time Tom got himself drunked up—and that was a long time coming, considering the shape you left him in— she met him at the front door with a shotgun and swore she'd kill him if he ever raised a hand to her or the kid." Jesse smiled at the memory, and there was a meanness in the expression that Webb despaired to see. "I guess he must have seen the light. There was never any trouble after that."

Webb's mind reeled; he turned away from his younger brother, turned back. "My God," he whispered, taking his hat off and then immediately putting it on again. "All this time—"

"All this time, you've been looking over your shoulder, expecting a posse?" Jesse seemed to enjoy the thought. In fact, he hooted with laughter, and Webb might have punched him in the mouth if he hadn't sworn off violence a long time before. He hadn't used his fists or carried a pistol since that day on the Southern Star, when he'd left his own flesh and blood for dead, and he still didn't trust himself.

"You think that's funny?" he asked, his voice very quiet.

It was a warning, and Jesse caught on right away, for once. He paled and offered up a faltering, foolish smile. "Hey, Webb. It's me, Jesse. Your kid brother." He slapped Webb's shoulder. "Come on. I'll buy you a drink."

Webb had a thousand questions to ask, but he knew he would never be able to give voice to most of them. He'd confine his curiosity to Jesse himself, forget the old man and Tom had ever existed. As for the boy, Thomas Stratton III, well, he wasn't ready to think about him at all. "No," Webb said, "I'll buy *you* a steak. We have some ground to cover."

Jesse was pleased at the prospect of a free meal; he'd always been a hearty eater—the work was hard on the Southern Star and on any other ranch, hard enough to stoke any man's appetite, let alone that of a growing kid—and to Webb he looked a little down on his luck. No telling how long it had been since the boy had eaten anything but trail food, though from the look and smell of him, he hadn't been passing up the whiskey.

In the dining room of the Comstock Hotel, over slabs of beef cooked rare along with creamed corn and baked potatoes, the brothers gave abbreviated versions of their recent pasts. Jesse had left the Southern Star after a particularly nasty quarrel with the old man, and he'd been drifting ever since, stopping to punch cattle on some ranch or sign up with a trail drive whenever he ran low on money. He spoke wistfully of the home place, though, and Webb saw resentment flash in the boy's blue eyes when he said he was sure their father must have signed the land and livestock over to Tom Jr. by then.

Good riddance, thought Webb. He'd loved the land, of course he had, for he was a cattleman by blood, but he had a place of his own now, the ranch at Primrose Creek. He would build it into an enterprise to equal or even surpass the Southern Star, but that was where the similarity ended. He wanted children, sons and daughters, and if he was lucky enough to have them, he wouldn't pit them against each other the way Tom Sr. had done, that was for damn sure. Nor would he wear out three wives, planting them one by one in a desolate, windswept churchyard overlooking the muddy Missouri River, along with their many ill-fated babies, laid to rest in coffins no bigger than shoe boxes.

"Where'd you get the money to buy your own place?" Jesse wanted to know. He'd finished his steak and was starting in on a wedge of cherry pie.

Webb had saved a part of his wages ever since he'd begun drawing them when he was fourteen, and after leaving the Southern Star he'd hooked up with a couple of cattle drives out of Texas and Mexico. In time, he'd become a trail boss, and, as such, he'd gotten a percentage of the profits. He saw no need to explain all that to Jesse, who was apparently more inclined to squander whatever came his way. "I worked," he said. "I'm looking for some cowpunchers right now. You know of any?"

Jesse beamed. "Sure I do. I'll sign on. So will seven or eight of my friends, and a few strangers to boot, I reckon, if the wages are right."

"The wages are nothing fancy," Webb said, "but

there's a good bunkhouse, and I've hired on a woman to cook." It seemed an understatement of phenomenal proportions, describing Megan as "a woman to cook," but hers wasn't a name he wanted to bandy about. In some indefinable way, it was nearly sacred.

"You never married?" Jesse asked, between bites of pie.

Webb shook his head. He'd loved Ellie, and they both knew it. Hell, everybody in Montana probably knew. "What about you?" he asked, though he was sure Jesse hadn't gotten beyond the stage of chasing saloon girls.

"No plans to settle down," Jesse said proudly, as though he were the first man ever to come up with the idea.

Webb smiled to himself. "I see," he said, as a serving woman came and filled his coffee cup. "Well, you round up your friends when you finish up. I'll hire on every man with warm blood in his veins and a horse to ride."

Jesse nodded. He would expect special treatment, Webb supposed, being the boss's brother. No sense in disillusioning him too soon. In point of fact, Jesse would be expected to carry his own weight, just like all the others.

He finished his pie and had a second piece, and Webb watched with amusement while that went down Jesse's gullet as fast as the first one. Then, while Webb enjoyed his coffee, Jesse got to his feet, apparently restored. "Where do we meet," he asked, "and when?"

Webb had been lucky that day, and not just because of the reunion with Jesse, the brother he'd left behind.

He'd expected to have trouble hiring the men he needed, but now it seemed that fate was going to provide those, too. It made him uneasy when things just fell into place like that.

"I've got a room here," he said. "I'll talk to the men in the morning and buy breakfast for everybody who hires on. I'll get you a bed if you want one."

That smirk lifted one corner of Jesse's mouth again. "Oh, I've got me a bed for the night," he said. "But thanks anyway. We'll see you out front."

"Dawn," Webb warned, although he was in no real position to make demands. Most of the men in Virginia City were miners, unlikely to saddle up and head out to ride herd in the high country. He'd take whatever help he could get and be glad of it.

Shortly after Jesse had nodded and taken his leave, Webb finished his coffee, settled the bill, and took himself upstairs. In his room, he lit a kerosene lamp, kicked off his boots, and stretched out on the lumpy bed to read a book he'd brought along from home. Finding himself too groggy to focus his eyes, he finally undressed, turned down the wick, and lay down to sleep.

Instead, he thought about the Jesse he remembered from seven years ago. The boy had been sensitive and skinny, with a love for books as well as horses, and he'd tried desperately to gain the old man's approval, all to no avail. There was a cruel streak in Tom Sr., and the harder Jesse strove to prove himself, the less attention he was paid.

At last, Webb dropped off to sleep, and he wouldn't have been surprised to dream about the Southern Star, about the old man, about Tom Jr., about Ellie and Jesse, even about all those lost babies. God knew he'd had a hundred nightmares about them as a boy, dreamed they were calling to him, calling and calling, thin voices piping on the harsh Montana winds.

Instead, it was Megan McQuarry who haunted his sleep. Megan, with her copper hair and impossibly green eyes, her fiery spirit and quick Irish tongue. He awakened well rested and eager to begin the long, hard ride home to Primrose Creek. Back to Megan.

He was pleasantly taken aback to find Jesse waiting for him out in front of the hotel in the predawn light, his horse saddled and ready to ride. He was sober, incredibly enough, and so were the twelve men he'd recruited to sign on with Webb's outfit. All of them had halfway decent horses and enough gear to see them through.

Webb spoke with each one, and, although he disliked a fair number of them on sight, he was running low on choices. He had cattle and horses to round up and sell to the army, and he couldn't do that on his own.

Jesse at his side, Webb turned his own mount toward the mountains and rode for home.

He was back.

Megan's throat caught with the realization, and she watched from the patch of land she'd been clearing for a kitchen garden as Webb and a dozen men rode toward the house. His face was shaded by the brim of his hat, and yet she would have sworn he was smiling.

She schooled her own expression to one of schoolmarmish dignity, though not before she'd forgotten herself and raised both hands to make sure her hair wasn't coming down. While the other men made for the barn, there to stable their horses before staking their claims to spots in the bunkhouse, Webb and a young fair-haired cowboy rode toward her. Augustus, barking deliriously, came bounding around the side of the house and rushed to welcome his master.

The two men stopped at the edge of the garden and swung down from their horses. Webb was indeed smiling, Megan realized, but she didn't dare presume that she was the cause of his good spirits, the way he was wrestling the dog in greeting, so she kept her own expression solemn. Inwardly, however, she was overjoyed to see Webb again; a wild surge of happiness arose and danced in her soul.

"Looks like you've been hard at work," Webb observed, indicating the garden patch with a nod of his head. He was still smiling, as though he knew her own straight face was a ruse. Maybe he'd even guessed that she'd missed him sorely.

Augustus had settled down a little, though he still whimpered in delight. Fickle dog. He'd hardly let her out of his sight from the moment Webb left the ranch, and now all his attention was reserved for someone else. Megan gathered up her skirts, suddenly conscious of the bright green silk, once trimmed with feathers at the neckline and hem. She'd torn off the fripperies and rolled up the sleeves, but the gown still looked like what it was—a fancy woman's get-up, made for a stage, a dance hall, or some such place. She saw the boy looking at her with frank appreciation, though she was dirty from head to foot, and blushed. "I'll get supper," she said.

Webb's gaze narrowed as he took in her dress, and she thought she saw his jawline tighten a little. He nodded almost curtly. "That would be fine," he grumbled.

The young man elbowed him, and he started, first in a flash of temper, then in sudden amusement.

"This is my younger brother, Jesse," Webb said. "Jesse, meet Miss McQuarry, my housekeeper."

It seemed to Megan that Webb hesitated slightly at the word *housekeeper,* as if he wanted to say she was something more, but surely she'd only imagined that. She'd been working hard since Webb had left four days before, and she'd been outside swinging a hoe and picking rocks since noon. Little wonder, then, if she was getting lightheaded and perhaps a bit whimsical. "How do you do?" she said, addressing herself to Jesse. She was still painfully conscious of the dress.

Jesse flushed. Perhaps a decade younger than Webb and not so ruggedly built, he was handsome all the same, and in time he'd be the sort of man to turn women's heads, like his elder brother. "How do?" he responded.

Webb pulled off one glove and indicated the outbuildings. "The bunkhouse is over there," he said to Jesse. "Feed and water your horse, and put away your gear. Time you're washed up, I reckon Miss McQuarry will have something on the table for supper."

Jesse looked somewhat taken aback, as though he'd expected to sleep in the house, and Megan was a little confused herself. In her family, kin was kin. They deserved—and got—the best of everything, no matter how little there might be.

"Sure," Jesse said at last, and led his horse away.

Megan ran her blistered hands down the front of her dress, painfully aware of her appearance. If only she'd known when he was going to return, she found herself thinking, she might have bathed, dressed her hair, put on something pretty. . . .

What was she thinking? She was a housekeeper, not a wife or even a sweetheart. Once again, she touched her hair. Then, embarrassed, she turned and hurried into the house, her face hot.

She went to her room, washed quickly, exchanged her dress for the one simple print gown she owned, and did what she could with her hair. Thankfully, there was fresh-baked bread, and she'd put a pot of beans and hamhocks on the back of the stove earlier in the day. There were eggs, too, from Bridget's hens, brought over the night before by Trace and Noah and stored in a basket in the ice house.

She collected those and put them on to boil, opened several large cans of fruit from the kitchen shelves, and started some biscuits. She was rushing about the kitchen when she became aware of Webb standing just inside the doorway, his hat in his hands. There was a look of curious affection in his blue eyes.

"It's a little late in the year for a vegetable garden, isn't it?" he asked.

"It's only June," she said, flustered, dashing from stove to shelf to table and back again. "There are lots of things that will grow."

He shrugged, hung his hat on a peg next to the door, and stepped inside. His clothes were filthy, and he could have used a bath and barbering, but he looked spectacular to Megan just as he was. It made her pulse race to think that he'd be sleeping under the same roof again, as of that night. She probably wouldn't get a moment's rest.

He proceeded to the wash stand, the dog prancing happily along behind him, nails clicking, tongue lolling. Webb poured water from the pitcher to the basin and began soaping and splashing his face, scrubbing his hands. Megan stood frozen, watching him, and was nearly caught gawking, turning away just in time to avoid notice.

The cowboys began to wander in soon after, led by Jesse Stratton, and they greeted Megan politely with nods and murmured "ma'am"s. They'd done their washing down at the creek, most likely, and while they were still far too dirty for decent company, they were hungry and minding their manners, for the most part, at least. She caught a few of them casting surreptitious glances her way and reckoned they'd seen her in her costume in the garden. None of them dared to make comment, of course, and they took their seats in good order, Webb at the head of the table, and tucked into the food Megan set out for them.

Watching them eat while she brewed coffee at the stove, Megan reflected that Webb had been right— cooking three meals a day for so many men was going to be more work than she'd ever undertaken before. Oddly enough, she liked the idea; like the other McQuarrys, she didn't take to idleness.

When the meal was over, she fed the few scraps to Augustus, who had waited patiently, one eye open to monitor the proceedings throughout supper, stretched out on the hooked rug in front of the kitchen fireplace. The men thanked her modestly and took their leave, including Jesse, disappearing two and three at a time into the twilight, mugs of coffee in their hands, until she was alone with Webb.

"That was a fine meal," Webb said. He lingered at the table, watching her, the light of the lanterns glowing golden in his hair.

She found herself smiling at him. "Why does it always seem to surprise you, Mr. Stratton, when I do something well?"

He had the good grace to look chagrined. He even reddened a little, along that strong jawline of his. He needed to shave, and badly, but Megan realized she wanted to touch him, just the same. She was all the more careful to keep her distance.

"I guess you look more like an actress than a house-keeper," he said.

"I didn't know you had a brother," she replied, because his remark disturbed her, and not in an entirely unpleasant way, and she needed to change the subject.

He sighed. "Ah, yes. Jesse. I ran into him in Virginia City. Turns out he left home more than two years ago."

Megan began washing dishes in a pan on the long counter under the broad eastern window, where morning light would spill in, pink and gold, when the sun rose. "Home?" she asked very quietly. "You mean the family ranch up in Montana?" If he didn't want to answer, if the question was too forward, he could pretend that he hadn't heard.

"For me," he said without hesitation, "home is right here at Primrose Creek."

She was oddly pleased by his answer, even though she grieved for this land that had once been hers. "What made you leave there?" she pressed, scrubbing away at a plate and avoiding his eyes. What caused her to be so daring? Webb Stratton's past was his own business.

He was quiet for a long while. Then, with a sigh, he spoke. "Your family is close-knit," he said. "Mine is different."

She waited.

"We never got along, Pa and me. Tom, Jr.—that's our older brother—and I could hardly stand to be in the same room together."

She felt a kinship with Webb then, for, of course, she'd known her share of familial turmoil, too. "What about your mother?" she asked gently.

"My mother," he reflected. She dared to steal a glance at him, out of the corner of one eye, her attention caught by something in his tone, and saw that he was staring off into the distance, his hands cupped around his enamel mug. He seemed to see something far beyond the sturdy, chinked log wall of the house, something that troubled him a great deal. "She died when I was five, I hardly remember her. Pa married Jesse's ma, Delia, before mine had been gone six months—in all the time I knew her, I never heard him call her by her Christian name. She was always 'woman.'"

Megan couldn't help herself. She went to stand just behind Webb's chair, laid a hand lightly on his shoulder. Took solace in the fact that he didn't pull away. "What was she like? Jesse's mother, I mean?"

He smiled, but a shadow of sadness moved in his eyes. "Delicate. Pretty. Hardly more than a girl when she first came to the ranch. She lost several babies before she managed to have Jesse, then passed on of a fever when he was just three. We didn't have a woman in the house again until Tom, Jr., went back east and married Ellie."

Ellie. Something in the way he said the name left Megan feeling stricken. She waited, not daring to speak, but he didn't say anything more about his brother's wife.

"What about you, Megan?" he asked gruffly. "Do you ever miss the homeplace, back in Virginia?"

She thought of the farm in the lush and fertile Shenandoah Valley, of her beloved granddaddy, and her heart ached for all she'd cared for, and taken so for granted, and finally lost. Once, she would have responded as Webb had and claimed Primrose Creek as the place she belonged. Now, she wasn't sure she fit in anywhere at all, and she didn't know what to say in the face of that insight.

Webb pulled her down into the chair next to his, took both her hands, and frowned when he saw the broken blisters on her palms and the insides of her fingers. His touch was comforting, and, at the same time, it sent a current of dangerous longing surging through her bloodstream.

"You've been working pretty hard," he commented gently.

She turned her head, blinking. She wasn't going to cry. She *wasn't*.

Webb got up, fetched a towel and a tin of salve, turned her hands palms upward, and proceeded to apply the medicine.

"I—I would have been all right," she said.

His eyes were as ferociously tender as a spring sky when he looked up into her face. "You don't much take to being looked after, do you?" he asked.

She drew a deep breath. "It's been my experience that it's better to take care of one's self." Davy had taught her that, single-handedly. She supposed she ought to be grateful for the lesson, but she wasn't.

His gaze searched her face, probing in a way that peeled away layers of carefully guarded defenses and at the same time infinitely gentle. "That's a hard way to live. Believe me, I know."

She drew a deep, resolute breath and got to her feet. "I'm an actress," she said. "Sometimes I can even fool myself."

He stood and examined her hands again. They were covered in salve and none too steady. "Maybe it's time you stopped doing that. Fooling yourself, I mean. You don't need to run anymore, Megan. You're home."

"Home," she echoed, as though the word were strange to her. In many ways, she guessed, it was. It had meant so many different things during her short lifetime that she was no longer sure how to define it. "This is your ranch, Webb. *Your* home. Not mine."

He'd confided in her, and she wanted to tell him about Davy, about her rogue of a father and her poor, trusting young mother dying in a stranger's bed, but she couldn't make herself do it. She was too afraid of what she might see in his eyes if he knew the whole truth about her. Judgment would be bad enough; pity would be unbearable.

To her amazement, he lifted one hand and stroked her cheek once with the lightest pass of his knuckles. His smile was slight and sorrowful, there one instant and gone the next.

"I'm pretty tired," she blurted, for the things she felt in that moment terrified her, with him touching her that way. And caring. "I need to get some rest." And that was as much a lie as the rest of her life, she thought, because there was something about Webb Stratton that revitalized her, made her feel that she could do anything, as long as he was nearby. Why, if she'd chosen to, she could have hitched up a mule and pushed a plow all night.

"Me, too," he said. "I guess Augustus and I will turn in for the night."

She nodded, vastly relieved. "Good night, then," she said brightly, and glanced at the piles of dishes waiting on the counter.

Webb followed her gaze. "Leave those for morning," he said. Then he smiled. "That's an order."

She laughed, then saluted. "I wouldn't think of disobeying," she replied, and rose to put out the lamps before retiring.

Webb stopped her with a shake of his head. "I'll be up awhile."

She nodded, touched her hair again, and started toward her bedroom.

"Megan?"

She paused, turned to look back over one shoulder. "Yes?"

"Aren't you going to eat anything? You didn't have supper."

She'd entirely forgotten, in the hurry to prepare a suitable meal for fourteen hungry men. It amazed her, the way he noticed these small things—her missing supper, the blisters on her hands—and cared about them. During the hard years away from her family and the dark time in England before that, when she and Christy had had virtually no one except each other, she'd gotten used to keeping her chin up and toughing things out. "I'm not—not really hungry," she said, and that, at least, was true, because besides being stricken to the heart by Webb's kindness, she was also a little frightened. Depending on someone else could serve no purpose other than to weaken her, and she knew she would need all her strength to make any sort of place for herself in the world.

"Good night, then," he said.

Augustus snuffled and lay down on the hooked rug.

"Good night," Megan replied.

Inside her room, she closed her door and leaned against it, waiting for her heartbeat to slow down to a normal pace. Moonlight spilled through the window she valued so highly, silvering the floor, the narrow bed, her collection of useless theatrical dresses hanging on the wall. Through the panel behind her, she heard the stove lids rattle and knew Webb was banking the fire for the night. In a little while, he'd retire to his room upstairs, and she would creep out and finish the dishes. Then, with her work finished, she *might* be able to sleep.

She lit a lamp, exchanged her dress for a nightgown,

being careful of the salve on her hands, and sat down on the edge of her bed to take down her hair and brush it. Gradually, a feeling of quiet, rather than an actual lack of sound, descended over the house, and although Megan did not hear Webb's boots on the stairs, she knew he was exhausted, and she was sure he'd gone to bed.

She slipped out of the bedroom, found that the lamps in the kitchen had been extinguished and the fire in the stove had been banked. She was midway across the room when she realized she wasn't alone—maybe it was a sound, maybe it was a feeling, but she knew.

She turned, and there, before the fireplace, where the hooked rug had been, stood a large tin bathtub, and Webb Stratton was lounging in it, one long leg stretched out over the edge. He was smoking a cheroot, and light from the hearth gilded his hair and lent a golden aura to his bare flesh.

Megan might have escaped unnoticed—he appeared to be lost in thought, gazing up at the ceiling—except that she gasped. He heard her then and turned his head. His grin shone like ivory in the night.

"Well, now, Miss McQuarry," he asked cordially, "what would you be doing out here? Not washing dishes or anything like that?"

Every nerve in her body was screaming for flight, but she couldn't move. She might have stepped into a patch of hot tar, so thoroughly was she stuck to the floor.

She saw one of his eyebrows rise.

"Miss McQuarry?" he prompted.

She managed to suck in a breath, and that steadied her a little, though her hands were knotted in front of her and her heart was trying to beat its way out of her chest. "I didn't realize you—you were here."

There was laughter in his voice, and though it was the friendly kind, Megan wasn't reassured. "I don't guess you did."

She tried to move and found that she was still frozen in place. Her knees felt dangerously weak, as though they might give out at any time, and her head was spinning. "I—well—you might have had the decency not to bathe in the kitchen!" she cried in desperation.

"It's my kitchen," he pointed out reasonably and without rancor. "Did you know the moonlight is coming in through the window over there behind you?"

She looked back and realized that her shape was almost surely visible through the fabric of her nightgown. She gasped again, clasped both hands to her mouth in mortification, and dashed for her room, slamming the door behind her.

Even then, she could hear Webb out there in the kitchen laughing. *Laughing,* the wretch. Just then, she didn't know which she wanted more—another look at Webb Stratton in the altogether or sweet, swift revenge.

Webb settled deeper into his bath, grinning long after his laughter had subsided. What a marvel Megan was, he thought. On the one hand, she seemed tough and independent, scrappy enough to take on an army of buzz saws, but there were broken places inside her, too. Private wounds that might never heal.

His grin faded. He'd been down that road with Ellie.

A reasonable man would keep his distance, find himself another woman to think about. Trouble was, when it came to Megan McQuarry, he wasn't a reasonable man.

Chapter

6

Gus set the vented wooden crate on Megan's freshly swept kitchen floor, beaming as he lifted the lid to reveal a swarming, silky, yellow mass of chirping chicks inside. She felt a deep fondness for the big man, watching as he knelt in the midst of all those tiny birds, picking them up so gently in his huge hands.

Augustus, proving himself to be of sterling character, barked once, cheerfully, came over to sniff the milling crowd, and then gave a huge huff of a sigh and went outside. No doubt rabbits would present a more interesting challenge.

Megan crouched with Gus, delighted by the baby chicks. Together, she and the storekeeper put them back into their crate by the handfuls. How, she wondered, would she ever be able to *eat* one of these dear creatures, even when they were big and ugly with their downy tufts turned to stubby feathers?

Gus seemed to read her expression with uncanny accuracy. "Is all right, miss," he said in his broad

German accent. "In time, more chicks come. Always more chicks."

Megan was mildly reassured—after all, it would be a while before any of these sweet, messy little critters were real chickens.

"You give them water," Gus went on, "and the feed I brought. Keep them warm, back of the stove, until they can be outside."

Megan nodded, and Gus left the house to bring in a bag of finely ground corn meal. While he was doing that, Megan set the box of cheeping fuzz at a comfortable distance from the cookstove and put a shallow pan of water in with them. She had helped with the chickens at home in Virginia, she and Skye, and she knew they might drown in too much water or get themselves wet, fall sick, and die. Many of them would simply not survive, no matter what she did, but that was unavoidable. Chicks and puppies and colts perished with alarming frequency, as did human babies, and there was no changing the fact, no comprehending the mystery.

"You make garden," Gus observed, pleased, when Megan insisted that he sit down and have a cup of coffee before heading back to town. "You grow vegetables? Flowers, maybe?"

Megan smiled. "Just pole beans and some lettuce this year, I think. A little squash, too, and some pumpkins for pie." She sighed. "It's late for planting," she said, recalling Webb's comment the day before.

"Well, is fine-looking patch," Gus said. "Next year, you get early start. Grow everything."

Megan allowed herself the luxury of believing that

she would still be at Primrose Creek come the spring, if not in this house with Webb on this land she loved so deeply, then somewhere nearby.

"Yes," she said, a bit belatedly. "Everything." Meanwhile, the chicks kept up their busy chorus. "Thank you, Gus."

His smile was the smile of a loyal friend. "You have such sorrow in your eyes, miss," he said. "You are home now. You should not be sad."

Home. The mere word filled Megan with such a sense of bleak yearning that, for the moment, she was tongue-tied.

"I just remember," Gus boomed, flushed with cheerful chagrin, patting his shirt pockets and then producing a folded slip of paper. "I bring message."

Frowning, Megan reached for the paper, unfolded it, and drew in her breath. The thin vellum stationery bore the distinctive name of Lillian Colefield— Diamond Lil.

Dear Miss McQuarry, she'd written. *I have decided to go ahead with plans to build my theater. I would like to call on you and discuss the idea, at your convenience. While I realize you may never wish to accept my offer of a leading place in the troupe, I find myself in need of advice. Please respond through Gus. Best Wishes, Lil.*

Megan was more than a little intrigued. While she had no desire to act again, and certainly no inclination to travel, she did love the theater itself. It would be nice just to *talk* about plays and sets and music with someone who shared the interest. Quickly, she found a slip of paper and a pencil and wrote her reply:

Miss Colefield,

I would be delighted with a visit. Please call any after-noon this week.

Megan McQuarry

When she'd handed the note over to Gus, he said his good-byes and left the house, stopping in the dooryard to speak to Augustus and ruffle his ears.

Once he'd gone, Megan peeled potatoes for supper, to be served with boiled venison and several tins of green beans. She was setting the table when she heard a lone rider, and, expecting Webb, she hurried to the doorway before she could stop herself.

The rider was Jesse, not Webb, and he grinned and swept off his hat when he saw Megan on the threshold, shading her eyes from the glaring rays of a sun fighting its inevitable descent toward the western horizon.

"Is everything all right?" she asked.

Jesse nodded. He was harmless, she knew, even sweet, but all the same, she didn't care for the way his gaze strayed over her body before wandering back to her face. She'd seen that look too many times, in the eyes of too many different men.

"Yes, ma'am," he said. "Webb sent me on ahead to tell you he's hired a couple more men. They'll be coming to supper."

She stepped aside to let Jesse enter the house, feeling shy. He moved past her, hat in hand, his neck glowing red.

"That dress you were wearing yesterday was really something," he blurted out, standing with his back to the fireplace. Then he went crimson to his hairline and looked so flummoxed and so very young that Megan felt sorry for him. "Fact is, I've never seen a cook like you. The ones I knew had full beards and bellies like barrels."

Megan laughed. "Thank you," she said. "I'm obliged—I think." She had guessed by then that Jesse was a little sweet on her, but she wasn't bothered by the discovery. She wasn't afraid of Jesse—she'd turned aside the wooing of bigger, stronger men, let alone boys like him, many a time—but she certainly didn't want to lead him on, either. That would be unkind. "Would you like some dried apple pie? I baked several earlier in the day."

He'd heard the chirping and was staring toward the crate of chicks, frowning. "Chickens?" he asked.

If Megan had known Jesse better, she would have pointed out the obvious nature of such a question, but she still viewed him as a relative stranger, and she needed more time to size him up. "Yes," she said. "They're too small to be outside just yet."

Jesse had been raised on a ranch, Megan knew that much about him, but he must not have been in charge of chickens. He acted as if he'd never seen one before, except breaded and fried and served up on Sunday china. Approaching the crate, he crouched to look inside. He chuckled, watching the birds scramble about.

Megan felt protective, like a mother hen. If she'd had wings and a beak, she would have clucked and flapped until Jesse Stratton had backed off a little. "They're very fragile, you know."

Jesse withdrew his hand, turned his head, and grinned at Megan, still sitting on his haunches. He did look like Webb, she found that appealing, and there was something else about him, some quality strictly his own, that inspired trust. "Sounds to me like you're already getting attached to the little beggars," he said. "I reckon you ought to get a kitten, if you want something to fuss over."

Megan felt as though she'd been accused of something, which, of course, was silly. She opened her mouth, closed it again, and watched as Jesse's grin broadened.

At the sound of approaching horses, he rose to his full height. Megan patted her hair and smoothed her skirts, without being conscious of doing so until she saw the worried look in Jesse's eyes. Caught, she blushed.

"My brother loves a woman named Ellie," he said quietly. "Think twice, Megan, before you go giving your heart away to the wrong man. You might never get it back again." With that, he went out, and Augustus scrabbled after him to greet the coming riders with a symphony of joyous barks.

She heard Webb's voice in the dooryard, caught herself smoothing her hair and skirts again. He came in just then, and the two of them stood there, squared off like a couple of gunfighters ready to draw on each other, or a pair of old friends on the verge of embracing. Megan wasn't sure which.

"Feels like a storm brewing," he said, and Megan didn't know whether he was talking about a real spate of bad weather or the crackling charge arcing back and forth between them.

Jesse came back inside then, and Megan turned her back on both of them without a word and went on with her work. She heard Webb speak to his brother in an even but firm voice.

"Go look after your horse. You left him saddled, and you know better."

She felt Jesse's reluctance to obey, rather than saw it, but he respected his elder brother and did as he was told, spurs clinking with irritation as he strode out of the house.

"Something happen that I should know about?" Webb asked when he and Megan were alone.

She didn't turn to face him but stood at the stove, trying to look busy. As it happened, the meal was ready to serve. "No," she said, and as far as she was concerned, that was the truth.

"Megan," he persisted.

She made herself meet his gaze and smile. "For some reason," she said, "Jesse's worried that you're going to break my heart."

Webb wasn't smiling. "Why would I want to do that?"

She sighed. He wasn't going to let this drop, she could see that. "He didn't say you'd *want* to, and neither did I. He did feel called upon to remind me that it's Ellie you really care about, though."

He scowled, flung his hat onto a chair. "Damn it," he muttered.

"It's all right," Megan said, though it wasn't, of course.

"It isn't all right," Webb argued. "And you know it."

"Webb—"

"I can't seem to stop thinking about you."

Megan sank into a chair. "What?"

Webb thrust a hand through his hair, then strode over to the wash stand to roll up his sleeves, douse water into the basin, and soap up his hands. He looked back at her over one shoulder, his countenance as sober as that of a hellfire preacher. "Don't pretend you don't know how I feel, Megan."

She stared at him. "How *do* you feel?" she asked. Her heart was racing so fast, she thought it might leave itself behind, and she couldn't quite catch her breath, either.

"I'm—well—" He rinsed his hands industriously, dried them on the towel above the wash stand. "*Attracted* to you."

Attracted? Did that mean he cared for her as a woman, as herself and no one else, or did it mean that he simply wanted to lie down with her? She sank her teeth into her upper lip and waited.

He faced her. "I'm not saying I love you, Megan, because I'm not sure what that means anymore. Maybe that's what I feel, and maybe it isn't, but I sure as hell feel *something,* and it's driving me out of my mind." He crossed the room, and by then he was standing so close that she could smell the piney wind in his clothes, along with trail dust and horsehide. "I've always fancied myself a pretty fair judge of character," he said, "but you've got me in a tangle. Sometimes you seem as delicate as a blade of new grass. At others, you're stronger than I ever imagined any woman could be. There's so much I don't know about you, and I figure it might take a lifetime to find it all out."

His speech had struck Megan to the heart. "I wish I

knew what you mean by all this," she said, somewhat lamely.

Webb's face was still serious, though there was a mischievous light in his eyes. "I mean," he said, "that I want you to be more than my housekeeper."

There it was. Megan was dizzy with indignation and disappointment. "I may have been an actress, Mr. Stratton," she said in a furious whisper. "Some people might even say I'm a fallen woman. But I assure you, I am *not* a prostitute."

He blinked, then a crooked grin broke over his face. "I was never real good at declaring myself," he said. "I guess I thought you might be looking for a husband." He paused, cleared his throat. His eyes were twinkling. "After last night."

Megan was very conscious of the hired men shouting to each other outside, some still attending to their horses, no doubt, while others were washing at the creek. If any one of them overheard this conversation, she would perish from mortification. "That," she snapped, referring to the bathtub incident, "was an accident. I thought you were already upstairs asleep."

He chuckled, but there was something in his manner that both thrilled and alarmed Megan. Made her want to run, to him and *from* him, both at once. "It's not such a bad idea, you know," he said. "Our getting married, I mean."

Megan gaped at him. "M-married?" she echoed, utterly confounded. She felt like the last in a long chain of skaters, whipping first in this direction, then in that, never able to catch her breath or get her bearings.

He glanced toward the door. The first men were

about to come in and break the curious spell that had turned Megan's reason topsy-turvy. "I guess we ought to discuss this later," he said.

Damn him, bringing up a subject like that and then just leaving her dangling. Megan could have strangled him, but she wasn't about to let him see how badly he'd rattled her. She turned away and busied herself with the task of serving supper.

Once the men were eating, she filled a plate for herself, carried it outside, and sat down on an upended crate to eat in some semblance of peace. The evening was cool, and, although the day had been a sunny one, there were clouds gathering on the eastern horizon, black and low-bellied. About to give birth to a deluge.

Presently, Webb came out with coffee and pulled up another crate. Inside, the cowboys continued to consume their suppers, talking a little, not so reticent as they'd been before. They were beginning to feel at home at Primrose Creek, she supposed, just as she was.

"Rain coming," Webb said, nodding toward the clouds. "I reckon we'll be up to our ankles in creek water come morning."

Megan's heart was skittering. He'd probably forgotten all about asking her to marry him, while she'd hardly been able to think of anything else *besides* matrimony, ever since he'd proposed the idea.

"It makes sense," he said, as though the conversation had never been interrupted. "Our tying the knot, I mean. You'd have your land back, legal as church on Sunday, as a wedding present."

Megan nearly fell off the crate she was sitting on, and she'd forgotten her supper completely. Just when she thought he couldn't surprise her, he did it again. "You'd *give* me this land, when you refused to sell it outright?" she marveled. "Why?"

"Because I want something in return," he said. He spoke quietly.

She swallowed. "What?" she dared to ask, though she was sure she knew.

Not for the first time, he surprised her. "A wife. A child. A family," he said. "That's the deal. You share my bed until you've conceived. Boy or girl, it doesn't matter. After that, you can sleep in your own room again—if that's what you want. If we decided not to go on living together as man and wife, then I'd build another house, up in the high meadow." He nodded in that direction, toward the land bordering the tract Megan's granddaddy had left to her.

"You cannot possibly think," she said, "that I would let you or anyone else take my child."

"I feel pretty much the same way about the matter, as it happens," he replied reasonably. "Guess we'd just have to try to get along, wouldn't we? Either way, the land would be yours, not just on paper but in reality."

"Why—why me?" Megan asked, after a long and awkward silence.

He grinned. "Well," he said, "you're right here handy." He glanced around, as though looking for a bevy of women, just waiting to marry up with a high-country rancher. "And I don't see anybody else in line for the job."

Megan was glad she was sitting down, because if she'd been standing up, her legs probably would have given out. She stared at Webb. "Are you insane?

Getting married is not the same as hiring a cook or somebody to punch cattle!" Inside the house, a sudden lull descended, alerting Megan to the very real possibility that their conversation might be overheard, and she lowered her voice. "You shouldn't marry anybody unless you love them, or at least think you *could* love them, and from what I hear, the woman you love is already married to someone else."

The coffee mug stopped halfway to Webb's mouth, and the grin faded away like the last light of day. He got up, took Megan lightly but inescapably by the arm, and double-stepped her toward the banks of the creek, where wildflowers bent their heads to sleep. The occasional rainbow flash of a trout shimmered beneath the surface of the water, and the grass, bruised by their passing, perfumed the air.

"What the devil are you talking about?" Webb demanded. He'd let go of her arm, but he might as well have been a barrier, standing in front of her the way he was, because she knew there was no way past him.

"We've already discussed this," she reminded him tersely. "Her name is Ellie, and she's married to your brother Tom."

Pain flickered in Webb's eyes, was quickly subdued. "Exactly," he said. "She's married to my brother." It was neither a denial nor a declaration, but it was enough.

Megan knew what it was to watch a dream die, and she longed to put her arms around him, though she refrained. She had pain enough of her own; if she drew Webb close, she might absorb his as well, and the burden would crush her. She wanted to ask if Ellie had loved him back, but she didn't dare.

Unexpectedly, Webb cupped his right hand under her chin, raised her face, and bent to touch his mouth to hers. At first, the kiss was not a kiss but a mere mingling of breaths. Then he kissed her without reservation, and Megan's heart leaped into the back of her throat and swelled to twice its normal size. She rose onto her toes, and her arms found their own way around his neck, and she felt something like lightning run the full length of her body and reverberate in the ground beneath her feet.

When their mouths parted, the world around her had hidden itself in a pulsing haze, and Megan had to blink several times before things came back into proper focus. The first thing she saw was Webb's dear, earnest, handsome face.

"I've been wanting to do that for a while," he confessed, his voice gruff.

Megan felt a smile land on her lips as lightly as a butterfly. "How long?"

"Since you got off the stagecoach the other day," he said, and the grin was back.

Color climbed her neck. "There's so much you don't know about me."

He brushed a tendril of hair back from her temple with the tenderest motion of his fingers. "And there's plenty you don't know about me. With any luck, we can spend the rest of our lives getting acquainted."

She was tempted, so very tempted. She felt a powerful attraction to Webb Stratton, it was true, but what about love? She'd thought she loved Davy, and in the end, she'd come to despise him, as well as herself. That particular mistake had cost her dearly, and she couldn't afford to make another one like it. "I'm scared," she said with real despair.

He was holding her shoulders now, and behind him, the vanishing sun raised a spectacle of crimson and gold. "Don't be," he replied.

"It wouldn't be right. I'm not—there was—"

Webb's expression was so tender, so patient, that tears burned behind Megan's eyes. "There was another man?" he asked quietly.

She tried to speak, but in the end she could only nod.

He sighed, bent his head, kissed her again. "I'll make you forget him."

Megan realized she was gripping the front of his shirt in both hands, clinging to him. She forced herself to let go, because she'd made a vow long ago to stand on her own two feet, always. "That's not what worries me."

He drew her close, held her, and she felt his breath in her hair. Felt his heart beating against her cheek. "Then what does?"

She allowed herself to be held, and the sensation was like drinking cold, clear water after a long and parching thirst. Augustus had joined them at some point, and he whimpered, perhaps sensing powerful emotions, seeking reassurance. "Trusting again," she whispered. "Believing again."

He kissed her forehead. "That will come with time," he promised.

Augustus whined, still troubled.

"I'm all right, Augustus," Megan said, her voice muffled by Webb's chest.

Webb laughed and held her at a very slight distance. "If you won't say yes for my sake, say yes for my dog's," he said.

She touched his cheek. She wanted to give a husband what her sisters gave to theirs, and receive what they received in return. They loved their men passionately, all of them. Megan did not know if she loved Webb at that moment, or if she ever would, but she wanted to take the risk. She wanted a *chance* to have what Bridget, Christy, and Skye had, and here it was, but the stakes were high, and she didn't want to lose.

"What if it doesn't work?"

"It will," he said.

"But what if you're wrong?"

He sighed, but his expression was gentle. Amused. "Then you'll have your land back, and we'll have at least one child together."

"I'll never give up my baby," she reiterated.

"Good," Webb said. "Then maybe you'll never give me up, either. Say yes, Megan."

"Yes," she whispered.

"Louder."

"Yes."

"Yes!" he yelled.

"Yes!" she shouted, and then they laughed like fools, the two of them, there beside Primrose Creek. The cowboys had gathered in the yard, and when Webb lifted Megan off her feet and spun her around in celebration of their agreement, they cheered and hooted and whooped.

Megan glanced at them, noticed that Jesse stood a

little to one side, neither smiling nor clapping. A sense of foreboding shadowed her hopes briefly, like a cloud passing overhead, but she'd forgotten it a moment later. She had only to look at Webb again to lift her spirits.

He took her hand. "When?" he asked.

She wanted to go out and beat the brush for a preacher right then, but she had her family to think about. She would get married properly, wearing a decent dress, with her sisters, brothers-in-law, nieces and nephews, and Caney all in attendance. The whole town—the whole *world*—would know that she was Webb Stratton's wife. "Soon," she said. "I want to do this right, make proper arrangements."

He heaved a great and beleaguered sigh. The cowboys, except for Jesse, had lost interest in the scene and headed for the bunkhouse, where they would probably play cards, smoke tobacco, and swap tall tales. Augustus was busy chasing an invisible rabbit through the high grass, barking as though he were truly fierce. "All right," Webb said. "I'll bunk with the boys until you and I are legally hitched."

Megan was touched by his chivalry, even though she would miss his presence in the house. She understood his reasoning, though: by tomorrow, everybody for miles around would know that they were engaged, and he didn't want people assuming they were already sharing a bed. Of course, there were bound to be those who would think precisely that, no matter what precautions they might take.

Side by side, hands loosely linked, they started back toward the house. Jesse was still there, smoking and leaning against the outside wall, braced with one foot. He smiled, but she glimpsed both anger and sorrow in his eyes.

Webb stopped to speak to his brother, and Megan went on into the house, closing the door behind her. As she was clearing the table, she heard the rasp of raised voices, although she couldn't make out any of the words.

She was washing dishes when Webb came in. He nodded to her, then went on up the stairs, presumably to gather his gear. As she was finishing up, he came down again, carrying a bedroll and some clothes. By that time, it was dark outside, and she had a lantern burning in the center of the table.

"Those chickens of yours will be moving out one day soon, I hope," he teased, watching her from over near the door.

She laughed. The noise they made was incessant, and if she didn't keep the straw bedding in the bottom of their crate changed, they'd begin to smell in short order. "About the time we get married," she promised. "Provided the chicken coop is finished by then."

Webb smiled. "I'll see to it myself," he said. He'd started the project before leaving for Virginia City to hire ranch hands, but it was only partly complete.

She simply nodded, and then he was gone. The house seemed vast without him, but she'd had a long day of hard work, and she was soon in bed and asleep, dreaming sweet, private dreams.

She awakened to chirping sounds the next morning, well before the sun had risen. Smiling, she threw back the covers and got up. After dressing, making a visit to the privy, and washing her face and hands, she made a huge breakfast of salt pork and hotcakes. Soon the long table was lined on either side with hungry men, but Megan was aware only of Webb as she worked, pouring coffee, serving second and third helpings.

When the meal was over and all the men had gone, including Webb, Megan put the dishes to soak and spent the next half an hour tending to the chickens. After that, she did some washing down at the creek, hanging sheets, shirts, trousers, and socks on various low tree limbs and bushes to dry. That done, she found a hook and line, dug up some worms, and she and Augustus went upstream to fish.

They returned with enough for the midday meal, and the crisply fried trout and thin-sliced potatoes disappeared in short order. Webb had brought several rabbit carcasses, already cleaned and skinned, and Megan had a supper stew simmering on the stove before she'd washed the last of the dinner dishes.

She'd just gone down to sit by the creek, with a book purloined from Webb's fairly sizable collection, when a fancy surrey, drawn by two pure black horses, came over the rise on the other side, descended, and splashed across to stop perhaps twenty yards from where Megan sat.

She would have known her caller by her grand hat, parasol, and ruffled gown, even if Diamond Lil hadn't trilled a cheerful greeting.

Megan was pleased to see her, and so, evidently, was Augustus, who came back from his travels to welcome the visitor. Lil laughed, spoke affectionately to the dog, and thereby assured herself of Megan's lasting regard.

"I hope I'm not intruding," the other woman said. She was wearing cosmetics, but they were artfully applied, and the effect was attractive. Megan, who had worn paint herself on the stage, did not miss the stuff.

She linked her arm with Lil's and started toward the house. "Come along. I'll brew some tea."

Lil raised a perfect eyebrow. "Have any whiskey?" she asked. Then, at the look on Megan's face, she laughed out loud. "Just joking," she said.

They entered the house, and the chicks immediately let their presence be known. Lil walked over and peered down into the crate. "Cute little critters," she observed. " 'Course, they'll be mud-ugly in a month."

That was undeniable. Surely it was God's plan for full-grown chickens to be ugly. If they stayed cute, no one would want to serve them boiled with dumplings. "I've decided not to name them," Megan said, quite seriously.

Lil's expression was wry as she swept over to the table and gracefully installed herself in Webb's chair. "I'd say that was a wise decision," she said. "It's pretty hard to eat anything with a name."

Megan put on the tea kettle. The rabbit stew was simmering nicely, and the aroma was pleasant. She'd make cornbread to serve with it at supper. "I'm interested to hear your plans for the playhouse," she said. "Do you really think you'll be able to make it pay? Primrose Creek is a pretty small place."

"Sit down," Lil commanded. "You make me nervous, fussing like that, and that water will boil on its own, without you hovering."

Amused, Megan sat. She liked Lil for her distinctive

personality and bold—the townswomen would probably have said *brazen*—ways.

"Now," Lil went on when Megan was settled, "about the Primrose Playhouse. Everybody needs entertainment, and I think we'll get a lot of trade from the men down at Fort Grant. Too, the town's been growing ever since the fire. With more and more women coming to live here all the time, it seems to me there's call for culture."

Megan wondered about Lil's past, how such an obviously intelligent woman could have ended up running not just a saloon but a thriving brothel as well. Of course, she would never ask her, though she was dying to do just that. "Where would you get the performers? You'd want a good deal of variety, to keep people coming back."

Lil waved one elegantly gloved hand, making light of the matter even before she spoke. "Virginia City is full of singers and the like, and we can bring magicians up from San Francisco."

There it was again, the word *we*. Megan decided it was time to speak up. "Mr. Stratton and I have decided to get married," she said.

Lil's smile was slow and thoughtful. "Well, now," she said. "Some of my girls will be sorry to hear that."

Megan willed herself not to blush, although she couldn't be sure she'd succeeded without bolting for a mirror, and she wasn't about to do that. She had no idea how to respond to Lil's statement.

Lil, unlike Megan, was not at a loss for words. She gave a sigh worthy of the stage and said, "I suppose that means you won't be interested in becoming my partner."

Megan's mouth dropped open; she promptly closed it again. "Your partner?" The kettle began to sing on the stovetop, but she paid it no mind. Listening to Diamond Lil's proposal, she forgot all about the tea she'd been planning to brew and the laundry still hanging down by the creek.

Chapter

7

*M*egan was in a distracted state of mind after Lil took her leave and so did not remember the laundry until she heard raindrops spattering on the roof and rumbling at the windows. By the time she reached the edge of the creek, the skies had opened wide, and her hair and clothes were immediately drenched as she rushed from one bush and tree to another, bunching sheets and shirts and other articles into her arms.

Augustus, eager to help, dashed around her in circles, barking in delighted panic. Unable to see past the small mountain of sodden wash clutched in her arms, she tripped over him and pitched headlong into the grass. Unsure whether this was a game or a genuine tragedy, the dog yipped and licked her face a couple of times as she sat up.

She laughed at the absurdity of the scene, and so Webb found her, sitting in the rain, surrounded by clothes and linens, her head thrown back and her dress sodden. Alone, he swung down off his horse and came toward her, frowning at first and then joining in her laughter.

He hoisted her to her feet with one hand, then helped her gather the scattered wash. By the time they reached the shelter of the house, they were as wet as if they'd both tumbled into the creek with their clothes on. They dumped the laundry onto the table and then stood there staring at each other, until Webb came to his senses and went to build a fire on the hearth. Augustus was close at hand, always ready to be helpful.

"Go and change," Webb said without looking at Megan. "You'll catch your death. Besides, the sight of you soaked to the skin is not having a wholesome effect on my character."

She hesitated, then went into her room. When she came out twenty minutes later, her hair was down, and she was wearing one of her poorly altered dresses, a pink-and-green striped silk affair entirely unsuited to Primrose Creek.

Webb, stripped to the waist, was drying himself with a towel. His expression was rueful as he took in the stage gown, and there was a glint of amusement in his eyes. "Well," he said, "that's hardly an improvement, now, is it?"

Megan's attention was riveted to the clearly defined muscles of Webb's shoulders, chest, and belly, and she raised her eyes to his face only by supreme effort. She was just about to tell him he was a fine one to talk when a modicum of reason overtook her, and she somehow managed to hold her tongue.

"Come over here and stand by the fire," he said. "You're shivering." He was accustomed to giving orders, and Megan was *not* accustomed to taking them but this time she obeyed, drawn by the warmth of the blaze on the hearth and by Webb himself.

She went to stand next to him. "So are you," she contrived to say.

"I'll survive," he said. With that observation, he walked away from Megan and mounted the stairs, and she felt bereft, watching him go.

He returned promptly, wearing a dry shirt—not yet buttoned—and carrying a blanket. He wrapped her in the latter, pulled it snugly around her.

It was back, that rare tenderness that would be her undoing if she didn't guard against it. She tried to step away, but she couldn't, because Webb was still holding on to the blanket, and she was cosseted inside it.

"Where is everybody?" she asked, because she was adrift, and if she didn't find a way back to solid, ordinary ground very soon, she was surely lost. She was referring to Jesse and the others, though for the life of her she couldn't have clarified the fact. Her tongue felt thick, and her head was swimming.

Fortunately, Webb knew what she was talking about, and it gave her some comfort that he looked as unsettled as she felt. "I left the men with the herd," he said. "Cattle tend to get spooked in weather like this."

"Oh," she said, casting a glance toward the stove. "I've made stew for supper—"

"I'll take it out to them in the buckboard," he said.

So he was leaving, going back to the range, where he and the men had been gathering strays. His imminent departure was at once a good thing and a bad one, from

Megan's viewpoint. She was a moral person, if somewhat misguided at times, and yet she did not trust herself to be alone with Webb for much longer. Getting drenched in a rainstorm had only added to his appeal, and there was a heat burning low in her middle that had nothing whatsoever to do with the fire crackling nearby.

"You're dripping," she said.

He still hadn't let go of the blanket, but he looked down. "So I am," he agreed.

Just then, Augustus gave himself a mighty shake and sprayed them both with dog-scented water. Startled, they stepped apart, and that was probably fortunate, given the way Megan's heart was thudding in her chest. She turned hurriedly, removed the blanket, and knelt to bundle Augustus into the folds.

The animal shuddered and licked her face gratefully, and she embraced him. When she looked up at Webb, she saw an expression in his eyes that made her breath lodge like a spike in the back of her throat. For what seemed like an eternity, the two of them just stared at each other, Webb standing in front of the fireplace, Megan down on one knee, both arms around the shivering dog. Finally, Webb broke the spell by thrusting himself into motion, buttoning his shirt as he went.

"I'd better get the wagon hitched and head back out to the range," he said.

Megan could only nod.

Fifteen minutes later, after she'd poured some of the rabbit stew into a smaller kettle for her supper and Augustus's, Webb returned from the barn, looking like a gunslinger in his long, dark coat, his hat dripping rainwater. He collected the large pot of stew, along with the utensils and enamel bowls Megan had gathered, and left again.

Megan felt desolate, but she had the laundry, as well as Augustus and the chicks, to occupy her mind. She got busy, draping sheets and garments over chairs, along the stair rail, from the mantels in other parts of the house. When she'd finished, she added a few sticks of wood to the fire Webb had built, fetched her sewing basket, and drew up a chair. There she sat, stitching one of Webb's new shirts together, while the rain continued to fall.

The range seemed especially barren to Webb that afternoon as he drove the buckboard back to the herd, his horse tied behind, to join the men guarding the steaming, bawling cattle. There were around a hundred head, by his count—fewer than he'd hoped for, he had to admit—and he knew the army would buy all the beef he wanted to sell, at a respectable profit. At the moment, though, he couldn't seem to take much interest in the prospect, because his mind was full of Megan McQuarry.

Megan, wet and laughing in the grass. Megan, with her red hair down around her waist and her curves showing through her dress. Megan, wrapping a dog in a blanket as tenderly as if he'd been a child. It was, he reflected, a damn good thing he had responsibilities, because, if he hadn't, he would have been back home, doing his best to seduce the woman. He had an idea she wouldn't have resisted overmuch.

The sight of Jesse riding toward him at a trot came as a merciful distraction. He had few illusions where the boy was concerned—growing up under Tom Sr.'s roof had taken its toll on all three of his sons—but Jesse was still the only kid brother Webb had, and he cared about him.

"The marshal's out here checking the brands on your cattle," Jesse said, making no effort to disguise the contempt he felt for men who wore badges. "What do you make of that?"

Webb didn't see any reason to point out that Zachary would soon be family, at least by marriage. Jesse and the others surely knew he meant to marry Megan, but he felt no real inclination to elaborate. "It's his job," Webb said. The rain was a steady drizzle now, and cold. "There's been a lot of rustling in this country lately."

Jesse looked a mite pale and a bit on the edgy side, too. "He thinks you're a thief?"

"I doubt it," Webb answered, bringing the buckboard to a stop near the lean-to that sheltered the campfire. While he was unloading the kettle of rabbit stew, Zachary rode up, mounted on a fine-looking dapple-gray stallion. Like Webb, he wore a long duster, and he was soaked all the same.

He greeted Webb with a nod, ignoring Jesse's pointed scowl.

"Afternoon, Webb," he said.

"Zachary," Webb replied. "My brother tells me you're looking at brands. Nasty day for it. Jesse, I guess you've met the marshal."

Jesse didn't speak, though he pulled his hat down low against the rain and nodded an acknowledgment.

Zachary grinned and swung down from the saddle, tugging off his leather gloves as he approached, and extended a hand to Webb. Webb responded with a firm grip.

"My wife's going to plague me three ways from Sunday if I don't come home with news of Megan," the lawman said. "How is she?"

Webb's attention was temporarily diverted to his brother, who was still sitting there with his horse reined in, gawking. The kid's ears were practically dragging on the ground. "You got something to do?" Webb inquired.

Jesse opened his mouth, thought better of whatever reply he'd been going to make, wheeled his horse around, and headed back to the herd.

Zachary took off his hat and thrust a hand through his damp hair. "Something tells me that kid hasn't got much use for me," he observed with a grin.

Webb sighed and indicated the campfire, where a pot of coffee was bubbling away. "Give him time. He's got some problems trusting folks, and not without reason."

Zachary looked after the boy, his expression serious but otherwise unreadable, but he was smiling again when he met Webb's gaze. "About Megan," he prompted.

Webb couldn't help giving a broad grin; just hearing her name made him feel as if the sun had come out, even though the rain was coming down as steadily as ever and the sky promised nothing but more of the same. "She's well." He wanted to boast that she'd accepted his marriage proposal, but the news wasn't his to break, so he would wait until Megan had spoken with her sisters. "Holding her own."

Zachary laughed. "Never met a McQuarry who couldn't do that," he said.

The conversation lagged a little, so Webb threw in "Fair cook, too," for good measure.

"Now, that"—Zachary nodded his thanks as Webb handed him a cup of hot, bitter trail coffee—"is not necessarily a family trait. If Caney ever lassos Malcolm Hicks, I'll probably have to take up cooking myself. When it comes to getting a tasty meal on the table, my Christy's real good at other things."

Webb chuckled, sipping his own coffee and watching out of the corner of his eye while his men kept the nervous herd corralled as best they could. So far, there hadn't been any thunder to speak of, or lightning, either, but there was an ominous charge in the air, and Webb felt as edgy as his cattle. "Nonsense. The women in your family can do anything they put their minds to, and you know it."

Zachary gave a rueful, long-suffering sigh, but the happiness in his eyes was unmistakable. "I reckon that's so," he admitted.

"You having any luck tracking rustlers?" Webb asked.

Zachary heaved another sigh, and this one was somber. "Nope. Dan Fletcher lost twenty head just a week ago, though, and Pete Dennehy is out a whole string of pack mules." He shook his head. "I'll be damned if I can get a bead on this bunch."

It was discouraging, just thinking about the other ranchers' bad fortune. Twenty head of cattle were more than most folks could spare and still meet their bank notes and stay in business. Dennehy was known for the mules he raised for sale to the railroad and Western Union, and this would set him back, maybe even ruin him. Same with the others. "Sounds like you need some help," he said.

Zachary chuckled, without humor, and blew on his coffee in an attempt to cool it down a little. "Every man in this country seems to be working either in the mines or on the railroad. Not many looking to be deputized for two dollars a day."

Webb was sympathetic. It was pure luck that he'd managed to hire the men he needed to work the ranch. "I might be able to spare a few days," he said. "Maybe bring along a couple of the hands."

Zachary lowered his coffee mug and narrowed his eyes, not in suspicion but in disbelief. "You'd do that?"

"We're neighbors," Webb said. "Friends, I hope. When do you want to ride?"

Zachary studied the sky. "Doesn't look like the weather's going to clear up right away, but we'd better head out in the morning all the same. You sure you want to do this?"

"Yep," Webb replied, never one to waste words.

"Damn," Zachary marveled, grinning again.

"I guess that means you're pleased," Webb said.

"Damn!" Zachary repeated, even more cheerfully this time, and then he shook Webb's hand again with vigor. "Much obliged, Webb."

Webb nodded. His reasons for joining the posse weren't entirely altruistic, of course, and Zachary must have known that. Rustlers were a threat to all ranchers, and the smart ones would want to take hold and do something before things got worse.

The two men agreed to meet at Zachary's office in town first thing the next morning, and then Zachary tossed away the last of his coffee—with some relief, Webb thought wryly—and mounted up. He gave the brim of his hat a tug in farewell and then rode away.

Webb figured he'd stood around jawing long enough. He finished his own coffee—he wasn't real particular about the flavor, it was the jolt he liked—untied his horse from the back of the buckboard, and headed out to the herd. The sky was as heavy as before, and some of its weight had settled into the pit of his stomach.

Webb and the others had been gone two days when, in response to Megan's invitation, sent by way of Bridget's eldest child, Noah, her sisters arrived for a visit.

"You're getting married!" Christy cried when the announcement had been made, raising her hands to her cheeks, her gray eyes alight. She and Skye and Bridget had left their assorted children in Caney's care, and they were undaunted by the continuing rain.

"Yes," Megan said, as seriously, as primly, as she could.

"I'll be horn-swoggled," Bridget put in, removing her damp bonnet and shaking it by its ties before hanging it on a hat peg next to the door. "It didn't take Webb long to get the idea."

Skye beamed as she shrugged out of her cloak. Although Jake Vigil had had his financial problems in the past, especially after both his house and mill were burned in the fire that had swept through Primrose Creek two years before, he was a prosperous man, and Skye's well-made clothes reflected his success. Megan had yet to visit their house, which stood several miles downstream on the opposite side of the water; she'd had her hands full just keeping up with her work. "I'm so happy for you," Skye said, kissing Megan's cheek.

Skye, like Bridget and Christy, was gloriously happy in her marriage, and she seemed to assume that the same fate awaited Megan. Megan hoped she was right.

"Thank you," she said.

Soon, with the fire blazing, the chicks chirping, and Augustus snoozing on the hearth, the four sisters were settled at the table, cups of tea steaming before them.

"When's the wedding?" Bridget wanted to know.

"Have you set a date?" Christy asked at the same time. She seemed a little on edge—she usually was when Zachary was away—but she glowed with well-being.

"I wanted to speak with all of you first, before we went ahead," she said, looking from one to another. "I have your blessings, don't I?"

"Of course," Bridget said.

"We hoped this would happen," Christy added.

"What will you wear?" Skye asked, her brown eyes glowing with excitement.

Before Megan could reply to any of them, Bridget spoke again. "Gus just got in a length of lovely ivory silk," she announced. "I have some lace trim in my sewing basket—"

"And I have some pearls from a gown of Mama's,"

Christy added eagerly, but after a beat she flushed slightly and lowered her eyes. Jenny McQuarry, the woman Christy and Megan had believed to be their mother, had never seemed to bear them any particular affection. Now, they understood her a little better.

While Megan and Skye knew at least something about their origins, knew they were the twin daughters of a servant girl, Megan doubted that Christy and Bridget had made any such discovery.

Megan reached out, squeezed Christy's hand, then looked at each of her other two sisters, lovingly, one by one. "You've all been so kind—"

"How else would we behave?" Skye replied, the McQuarry pride staining her cheeks and snapping in her eyes. "You're our sister, and we love you. This is a great occasion." She paused, drew in a breath, and rushed on. "I will buy the silk, Bridget can contribute her lace trim, and Christy her pearls. We'll all do the sewing—make a day of it. How about tomorrow, at my house?"

Megan had been wanting to visit—Jake and Skye's house had been built after she left Primrose Creek— and she was touched to the soul by her sisters' eagerness to make her wedding day memorable. "Thank you," she said with a little sniffle, quickly quelled. "Thank you—all of you."

"We're glad to have you home," Bridget said, smiling.

"I told them about our mother," Skye confessed, a bit guiltily. "How we're twins and everything."

Bridget sighed. "It's all so strange," she murmured. "I still can't believe it sometimes."

Christy nodded in agreement. "All my life, I've thought Granddaddy hung the moon, and I still believe he did what he believed was best for us. Just the same, I lie awake sometimes, racking my brain for even a scrap of gossip I might have gleaned somewhere along the way—"

"Caney knows," Bridget stated quietly, and now there was a spark of fury in her cornflower-blue eyes. "She says she doesn't, but I can tell when she's lying."

Christy nodded again. Sighed. "All we can do is make sure *our* children know *us*," she said. "I've been keeping a journal, so that someday—"

Megan got up and poured more hot water into the plain crockery jar that served as a teapot. Webb would never have thought to purchase such a frippery when all he drank was coffee. Such was life in a bachelor's house. "I think that's a wonderful idea, keeping a diary."

"As long as you're not doing it because you don't expect to be around for a long, long time," Skye said, studying Christy narrowly.

Christy laughed. "We'll all live to be ancient," she said. "We've got Granddaddy's blood in our veins, remember?"

It was comforting to think of that. Looking around the table at each one of her three beautiful sisters, Megan could see their grandfather in all of them. "You're the reason I want to marry and have a family of my own," she said. "All of you, separately and together—I've learned what's truly important by watching you."

A silence fell, broken only by a few sniffles, quickly dispensed with.

"I still miss him so much," Skye confided, at some length, and her voice was, for that moment in time, the voice of the child she had been. "Granddaddy, I mean."

Bridget nodded. "Sometimes it seems as though he's still around somewhere, close by, looking after us. We've been through a lot, each one of us, and I'm not sure we could have survived without help."

Christy made a steeple of her fingers and frowned thoughtfully. "Granddaddy's with us, all right," she said after a brief pause, "but in here." She touched her heart. "He left us more than the land. We have his courage, and I don't care if that sounds vain." The look in her eyes dared them, or anyone, to challenge her, and they all smiled, because it only proved she was right.

After that, they discussed Megan and Webb's wedding, agreeing that it ought to be held right there, in the house the newlyweds would share. They made plans to begin work on the dress the next afternoon at Skye's and decided that Bridget should bake several of her coconut cakes to serve after the ceremony.

Twilight was coming on, and the rain had decreased into a soggy mist by the time they all got into Skye's surrey and took their leave.

Megan stood in the dooryard, the loyal Augustus panting at her side, until they were clear out of sight.

Then, feeling a little lonely with her sisters gone and Webb out riding with Zachary, she went back inside, lit more lamps, and put some leftover soup on to heat. She and Augustus would have their supper, and then she'd gather the damp laundry hanging all over the house, to be pressed in the morning. After that, since she had the house to herself, she would take a lovely bath in steaming hot water.

The plan went off without a hitch, but barely. She had just gotten out of the bath, dried herself, and put on a flannel wrapper, donated by Christy, when the door opened and Webb stepped into the kitchen, looking wet and exhausted. He glanced at the tub, still full on the hearth, and grinned in a way that tugged at her heart and made her want to fuss over him. "What are you doing here?" she asked. "I thought you were out with the posse."

"No luck," he said. "We'll be heading out again in the morning." He let his gaze drift over her. "I just wish I'd gotten back a few minutes sooner."

She rather liked his teasing, though she was enough of a lady not to admit as much, at least while she was standing there in a wrapper and nothing else, with her feet bare and her hair trailing, still damp, in spiral curls around her waist. She raised her chin and tried not to smile. "Have you eaten?" It was hard to be businesslike in such a state of dishabille.

"Had some jerky out of my saddle bags," he said. He took his sweet time, hanging up his hat, pulling off his leather gloves, shedding his coat. "It was no feast, but I'm full."

"Coffee, then?" she pressed, but cautiously.

He sighed. "That sounds fine," he said, and crossed to the hearth.

While she was brewing fresh coffee, he dragged the bathtub to the side door and emptied it into the mud, then hung it in its place again.

"Are the men coming in later?" she asked, getting a

mug down from the shelf, fetching the sugar she knew he liked to add.

Webb was in front of the fireplace again, crouching there, scratching Augustus behind the ears and murmuring to him. Augustus sneezed heartily, as if to let it be known that he, too, had endured a cold, wet, and difficult day.

"They'll be spending the night in camp," Webb answered. "I'll go and join them. I just stopped by to look in on you and say that I'm going back out with Zachary tomorrow. We might be gone several days this time."

Megan set the cup and the sugar bowl down on the table. She'd forgotten, by then, that she was not properly dressed, and later she would wonder about that. For the moment, she was busy worrying. "You're going to be a deputy?"

"Just until this business is settled," he reiterated quietly. "There's been a lot of thievery around here lately. Zachary needs help."

She could hardly beg him not to offer much-needed assistance to her sister's husband, but she wanted to. Her mind was spinning with images of Webb being shot or injured, or simply catching his death in the damp weather. "I see," she said, and bit her lower lip.

He smiled. "I'm glad you're here, Megan," he said gruffly. "I'd forgotten what it was like to have a woman around."

Megan blushed, though she knew his comment was not meant to be a disrespectful one. "There's—there's something I need to know," she said, taking herself by surprise. "Did she love you? Ellie, I mean."

He gazed at her steadily for what seemed a long time. Then he answered. "I thought so once," he said, and she believed him. "It was all wrong, though—I see that now, though I was too young and hotheaded back then to get my mind around the idea. A thing that's wrong at the start can't be expected to turn out right in the end, can it?"

She shook her head. "No," she agreed. "This is all so confusing—feeling these things—finding out that Bridget and Skye are my sisters—"

He arched an eyebrow, and she realized she hadn't told him about Granddaddy's elaborate scheme to keep his family together, and no one else had, either. While he sat at the table, sipping hot, fresh coffee, she explained it all, or what she knew of it, anyway.

At the end of the story, he gave a low whistle of exclamation. "A man's got to admire that kind of gumption," he said. "Seems like it skipped a generation, though—passed from your grandfather to you and your sisters."

"I always wonder about that. How such fine people as Gideon and Rebecca McQuarry could produce the sons they did."

He leaned over, kissed her lightly, innocently on the forehead. Harmless as it was, that kiss took fire and blazed through her blood. "And I'll always wonder," he replied, "how a son-of-a-bitch like my old man could have had a fine son like me."

They both laughed.

"Maybe we can make sense of things, if we work together," Webb said, more seriously. "What do you say, McQuarry?"

She almost said it then, almost admitted that she was beginning to love him, against all will and reason. The words welled up from within her, as if springing from the root of her soul, but she held them back. What did *she* know about love? She'd already proven herself to be anything but an expert on the subject, believing Davy's lies the way she had. "I say we ought to try," she answered very softly, and she knew her eyes were shining, that she hadn't entirely hidden what lay in her heart.

"I'd better go," he said, nearly sighing the words. "Do you know what a temptation you are, in that nightgown, with your hair down?" He let a strand slide between his fingers. "Soft."

Megan closed her eyes, swayed slightly. What was it about this man that made all the strength in her body seep down into her feet and then soak into the floor? No one, certainly not Davy, had ever affected her in such a way.

He kissed the top of her head. "Good night," he said, and stepped back.

"Good night," she managed. She didn't want him to go, not because she was frightened of being alone, not because she would be diminished without him, but because she was so much more vividly alive when he was nearby. He brought a shape and a substance to her life that simply were not there without him.

He cupped her cheeks in his hands. "I could stay."

She called upon all her McQuarry determination. She wanted their marriage to be right, from the first. "Better if you go," she said.

His blue eyes were remarkably tender as he looked

down at her, and at the same time they blazed with a heat that rivaled the flames on the hearth. "You're right," he said with a sigh. "I hate to admit it, but you're right."

Having said that, he bent his head and kissed her with a sort of reverent hunger. Once again, the floor undulated beneath Megan; once again, she held on to the reins of her emotions, but they were slipping. Fast.

"Go," she gasped when she drew back.

He nodded, went back to the door, and took his hat and coat down from the pegs on the wall.

Megan's head cleared, and she remembered that he was rejoining the posse in the morning. "You'll be carrying a gun, won't you?"

"I can borrow a rifle from Zachary if I need one," he said.

She nodded. "Be safe," she said.

He didn't answer, didn't promise he wouldn't be hurt, and that troubled Megan, irrational as it was. Of course, he couldn't make a vow like that—no one could—but she still wanted to hear it. She wanted to storm the gates of heaven itself, pounding with her fists, demanding to know that no bullet would find Webb Stratton while he searched for rustlers or at any other time.

When he'd gone, she latched the door, put out all but one lamp, and retreated to her room, with its narrow, lonely bed. Augustus padded after her and curled up on the floor at her side with a long and philosophical sigh. She was deeply moved, sure he sensed her loneliness and wanted to lend what comfort he could.

"He'll be all right," she told the dog, rolling onto her side and bending down to stroke his silken coat.

Augustus whimpered, as though he had his doubts, but his presence was comforting to Megan, and she soon drifted off to sleep.

She awakened to a low growl and sat up, blinking. She'd secured the main door, but there was someone in the house, all the same. Webb? No—Augustus would have gone to greet him; instead, he lay on his belly, forelegs in front of him, making that grumbling sound.

Before she could arise, she saw a man's form take shape in the shadows of her doorway—she'd left it open in case Augustus wanted to leave again during the night—and although a scream rose in her throat, she strangled on it. She was literally too frightened to cry out, or even to move.

Augustus's growl turned to a snarl. He raised himself onto his haunches, and even in that thick darkness, Megan could see that his hackles were up. His teeth gleamed, more ominous than the fangs of a snake.

The shadow man stiffened. "Settle down, boy," Jesse said. A gun whispered against leather as he drew.

"Jesse?"

Augustus slumped to the floor, but Megan was still annoyed, and frightened, too.

"No," she said, urgently and with force. "If you kill this dog, Jesse Stratton, you'd better be ready to kill me, too."

She heard the pistol slip back into its holster. Augustus didn't move, but Megan knew he was poised to spring. Knew he would have gotten himself shot in the attempt to protect her, the dear, foolish thing.

She sat up, pulled on her wrapper, struck a match, and lit the lantern on the little table next to her bed.

Sure enough, Jesse was standing in the doorway. "I didn't mean to scare you," he said, and, remarkable as it was, Megan believed him. He looked pale and sick, and that aspect of his appearance alarmed her more than any threat to her own safety could have done.

"What is it?" she demanded, bolting to her feet. "Has something happened to Webb?"

Jesse thrust a hand through his hair, in a gesture very reminiscent of his older brother. "No," he said. "Not yet."

"What do you mean, not yet?" Megan reached down to stroke Augustus's head, hoping to calm the animal, but she was far from calm herself, and the dog must have sensed that. Like a child, he took his cues from what she did, not what she said.

"It's all a trick," Jesse said miserably. "All of it."

Megan's stomach dropped, bounced into the back of her throat. "*What* is a trick, Jesse? Damn it, *tell me.*"

"Those men Webb hired. My friends. It's them Webb and the marshal have been looking for. They're here to steal the herd."

Chapter

8

Megan's heart lay heavy and cold, half frozen with fear. For a long moment, she was so furious, so stricken, that she couldn't say a word to Jesse, but, being a true McQuarry, she soon found her tongue. She thrust both palms hard into his chest, not giving a damn that he was half again as big as she was.

"You betrayed your own brother?" she demanded. "How could you do a thing like that? Webb trusted you, welcomed you. He gave you a job!"

Jesse looked downright gray, and even younger than he was. His eyes seemed huge, and his Adam's apple bobbed as he swallowed. He was obviously ashamed, and remorseful, too, but as far as Megan was concerned, the damage was done. "I'm sorry. I didn't think—"

"You didn't think," Megan mocked, shoving him backward into the kitchen, toward the main door. "Damn you, Jesse, if I had the time, I swear I'd take a buggy whip to you. You go out to the barn and saddle a

horse for me—this instant—and don't give me any backtalk!"

Jesse backed, blinking, over the threshold, into the damp, windy night. "A horse? You can't—"

She pushed him through the opening and slammed the door in his face. "Saddle that horse! Now!" she yelled through the heavy panel, then hurried back to her room and began pulling on the first clothing that came to hand, a black velvet evening gown, trimmed in pink sateen, that she'd worn on the stage. It was highly impractical for the task at hand, and heavy, too, but it would provide warmth and a degree of shelter from the weather. As she dressed, she regretted being so prideful as to refuse her sisters' repeated offers to lend her clothing.

When she and Augustus reached the barn, perhaps ten minutes later, Jesse was leading out a little bay mare, chosen from the string of horses Webb kept to train and sell. Even in the relative darkness, she saw the startled expression on Jesse's face when she mounted, nimble as a monkey, Webb's rifle in one hand, and nudged the mare into motion with her knees.

"Where the hell do you think you're going?" Jesse shouted through the rising wind. The rain had stopped for a little while, but Megan knew the worst of the storm was yet to come.

"Never you mind where I'm going," Megan yelled back. "You go and fetch Jake Vigil," she said, pointing to the rise on the other side of the creek. "Then Trace Qualtrough. Tell them what you told me."

Jesse was trying to mount up, too, but the process

was a protracted one, since his slat-ribbed sorrel gelding had turned fitful and taken to dancing a fancy side-step that had Jesse hopping along with one foot in the stirrup and one still on the ground. "You're heading out to the herd!" he accused, as fresh, ice-cold rain began to slice down upon them. "You let me do that. *You* go fetch those fellers, whoever they are!"

"Do as I tell you," Megan called over one shoulder, reining her horse westward, toward the place where Webb had told her the herd was gathered, "and maybe I'll try to talk the judge out of hanging you for thieving!"

She thought Jesse might pursue her, and maybe he considered it, but when she reached the edge of the woods and looked back, she saw him and his horse splashing across the creek. She prayed he would obey orders——having no real reason to believe he would—— because she was going to need Jake and Trace's help to stop those rustlers from driving off the herd. She wished she had her own mare, Speckles, but she, like the land, had been sold long ago. As she rode, she silently cursed the day she'd laid eyes on Davy Trent.

Because the sky was overcast, Megan could barely see, but she followed Augustus, who made an intermittent yellow flash as he ran through the trees. She was slapped and battered by low-hanging branches as she raced on, moving as fast as she dared, and once, when the mare stumbled in a ditch, she nearly dropped the rifle. Her teeth were chattering, mainly with cold, though she might have admitted to a measure of fear, depending upon who was asking.

Thunder began to rumble as she rode higher and higher toward the top of the ridge. Sure enough, the herd was there, sheltered in the small canyon below, and when she gained the vantage point, lightning spiked across the sky and danced on the ground, illuminating the milling cattle and the rustlers in a series of brilliant, blue-gold flashes. Augustus hunkered down on the wet ground, growling.

"Quiet," Megan commanded, though there was no likelihood that he'd been heard.

The terrified cattle were bawling fit to raise the dearly departed, churning round and round like whirlpools in a flooded river, and the men riding herd shouted to each other in hoarse, worried voices. With every strike of lightning, every boom of thunder, the creatures, two-legged and four-legged alike, became more agitated.

Megan thought of the discussion she'd had with her sisters that afternoon and hoped they'd been right, figuring that Gideon McQuarry was still looking after them all, from wherever he was. "Granddaddy," she murmured, "if you're listening, if you're looking on, I need your help, and I need it pretty quick."

There was no blinding insight, but it did come to her that Granddaddy had always believed in action. *Do something,* he'd often said, only half in jest, *even if it's wrong.*

Her arm was aching from the weight of the rifle— there was no scabbard on her saddle—so she rested the weapon across the pommel, in order to balance it while she descended the hill. Augustus, perhaps heeding her instructions to keep his own counsel after all, perhaps merely as frightened as she was, trotted alongside, nose skimming the ground every now and then.

It hadn't occurred to Megan that if the lightning had revealed the herd and the rustlers to her, the reverse might be true as well. When the whole hillside lit up and the herd began to scramble through the opening of the canyon, the cattle trampling and goring each other in the process, she saw two men riding up the trail toward her. At the rate they were traveling, there was no question that they'd seen her and that their intentions were bad.

Well, Granddaddy, she thought, with resignation, *I did something, like you said, and it was wrong.* Then she raised the rifle, cocked it, and sighted in. She didn't like the idea of gunning anybody down, for any reason, but she'd do it if she had to, to stay alive.

The cattle began to run, bellowing now like souls being driven into the flames of hell, and Augustus shot forward like an Indian's arrow, racing toward the approaching riders, barking.

The dog was sure to be killed, and Megan knew that even if she was lucky enough to live through this night, she'd never forgive herself. She'd had few enough friends in her lifetime, and Augustus had been one of the best.

Her finger was on the trigger, ready to fire, when another bolt of lightning revealed that one of the riders was Webb, and the other was Zachary. She was so relieved, and so utterly horrified by what she had nearly done, that she didn't release her grip fast enough when she lowered the rifle, and a shot pinged into the ground.

The mare, already scared halfway out of its hide, reared straight up, pawing at thin air as though to claw a hole in it, and sent Megan slipping backward to topple over its rump and land with stunning force on what should have been soft ground, even mud, given the recent rain. Conscious of the danger of being kicked or dashed to shreds under those panic-driven hooves, she hurled herself to one side, bruising herself even more as she rolled over the fallen rifle.

Before she could get her breath, Webb was kneeling on the ground beside her, pressing her down by the shoulders when she tried instinctively to rise. "Are you hurt?" he roared. She wasn't, but it might not be prudent to say so.

Megan hesitated as long as she could, but her mental inventory had already indicated that she was just fine. "No," she said. "No, I don't think so."

Webb got up then and, taking one of her hands, wrenched her unceremoniously to her feet. "Then go home! It might have escaped your notice, but we're just a little busy here!"

Megan seethed. Remarkable, she thought. Here she'd risked life and limb, trying to save *his* blasted cattle, and how did he repay her? By jerking her up off the ground and shouting at her. "I'm not going anywhere!" she yelled back, just on general principle. Heading for home was the reasonable thing to do, she supposed, but she felt anything but reasonable just then. She was mad enough to spit. "Jesse just told me that the men you hired are rustlers!"

Webb bent down so that his nose was almost touching hers. "I already know that," he growled. "Now get your bustle back on that horse and *go home,* or I swear I'll take you across my knee right here!"

Zachary had caught and settled the anxious mare, and he led it over to her. "We've got our hands full here, Megan," he said, "and the best thing you can do to help is stay out of the way, so we don't have to worry about you."

The rain started again just then, with fresh force, and Megan felt as though someone had upended a bucket of cold water over her head. She ached in every joint and muscle, and she was mortified into the bargain. She wasn't a man, that was true, but she could ride and shoot as well as most of them, and Webb needed her help—he was just too hardheaded to admit it. On top of that, he wasn't even grateful that she'd tried to save his mangy cattle from a pack of rustlers.

By that time, the herd was in full stampede. In that rugged country, they could easily kill or injure themselves; probably a number of them already had.

Megan looked from Zachary's face to Webb's, which was hidden by the night and the brim of his hat, then turned in defeat, gripped the saddle horn, and mounted the mare. Zachary handed up the rifle.

"How did you know?" she asked. "About the rustlers, I mean?"

"Figured it out the other day, when I was checking brands," Zachary answered. "Listen, Megan, maybe you ought to pass the night with Christy. Tell her we'll be all right."

Tell her we'll be all right. The words echoed in Megan's mind as she watched the two men get back on their horses and head straight for the heart of chaos. *Tell her we'll be all right.*

"They'll be *all right,*" Caney said half an hour later

when Megan was seated before the kitchen stove in Christy's kitchen, wearing one of her sister's nightgowns, wrapped in a heavy blanket, and still shivering so hard that her teeth chattered. Instead of following his master, Augustus had accompanied her on the ride through the trees and over the creek, evidently following some canine code of honor, and Christy was drying his coat with one of her good towels.

She looked pale—naturally, she was worried about Zachary—but her gray eyes were fierce with anger. "What were you thinking of, Megan McQuarry, chasing off after a pack of outlaws all by yourself like that?"

Caney handed Megan a cup of tea, laced with honey and a dollop of whiskey, and tried to hide a smile. "I reckon she thought she was going to help some way," she said, in her smoky voice. "Didn't you, girl? I declare, you'd have been better off, the four of you, with a little less of your granddaddy's cuss-headedness."

"I couldn't just sit there at home and do nothing, knowing Webb was about to lose everything," she said, well aware that it was a lame excuse. Nonetheless, it was all she had. She looked at Caney, then Christy. "Could I?"

"*You* wouldn't have, if you'd known," Caney told Christy.

Christy's eyes glittered with tears. "It's bad enough that I have to worry about Zachary all the time. I don't need to be fretting over my sister, too!"

Caney's smile broadened, but there was something broken in it, something fragile. "Seems to me you ought to have some of this doctored-up tea, too," she told Christy. "Come on and sit by the fire, and give that poor dog some peace. You keep rubbin' him like that, you're going to wear the skin right off him."

Christy's hair was trailing down her back. She was clad in a heavy nightgown, a flannel wrapper, and a pair of Zachary's woolen socks, and still she was beautiful enough to attend the ball at some castle and distract the Prince from Cinderella for good. She got to her feet and did as she was told, and Caney handed her some tea of her own. "I don't know why I had to fall in love with a lawman," she fussed. "Why not a farmer, or a banker, or a storekeeper?"

Caney laughed, but, even in her present state of mind, Megan saw the sorrow in her friend's eyes. "We don't choose love," she said. "Love chooses us. And it don't much matter what our druthers might have been."

Megan took a steadying sip of the stout, blood-warming brew, and though it seemed that her spirit had stayed behind on that hillside with Webb, her heart went out to Caney. "I guess things aren't going too well with Mr. Hicks," she said softly.

Caney sighed and joined Christy and Megan at the table. "He's a stubborn man, my Malcolm." Megan saw tears in Caney's eyes, and that was a rare occurrence, despite what they'd all been through over the past decade or so, what with the war, and Granddaddy dying, and the farm being lost to Yankees. "I'm at my wit's end, where he's concerned. I tried cookin' for him. I tried fussin' over him. I tried ignorin' him. And nothin's changed, nothin' at all."

Both Christy and Megan were still, sensing that

something was coming, something about to break over them with as much force as the storm tearing the night sky asunder. Neither of them wanted to hear, but they could no more prevent it than they could change the weather.

Caney blinked and dashed at her eyes with the sleeve of her woolly robe. Her gleaming, abundant hair was subdued into a crinkly braid, thick as rope, and for what might have been the first time in her life, Megan saw her clearly. Because Caney had cared for her and for her sisters, because she'd been at the farm as far back as any of them could remember, they'd thought of her as old. Now, Megan realized that Caney probably wasn't even forty, and that she was beautiful.

"Any sensible man would be proud to have you for a wife," Megan said, in a hopeless effort to forestall the inevitable.

"About time I moved on," Caney said. "Three of you are married, and you're spoken for, Miss Megan. Webb's a good man, and he'll make a fine husband." She smiled a misty smile. "I wouldn't make a habit of crossin' him, though, if I was you." A throaty chuckle. "But then again, if I *was* you, I probably would."

Both Megan and Christy had stiffened in their chairs, and they were both weeping silently and without shame.

"None of that," Caney scolded. "I done spent my life lookin' after you four. It's my turn to kick up my heels."

"Why can't you stay at Primrose Creek?" Christy asked, making no attempt to dry the tears on her cheeks. "You can kick up your heels all you want, right here."

But Caney shook her head. "I love Malcolm Hicks. Love him with my whole heart. I can't stay because I can't bear seein' him all the time and knowin' he don't think enough of me to make me his wife."

Megan and Christy looked at each other in despair, but neither of them had any idea how to respond. No matter what joy the four McQuarry women might find with husbands and children and each other, Caney's going would leave an empty spot in each of their hearts.

Megan reached out to take one of Caney's hands, and Christy took the other. And they just sat there, the three of them, holding on and, at the same time, trying to let go.

Megan awakened in a twist of sheets, soaked in perspiration and gasping from some dreadful dream, still crouching like a monster just beyond the reach of her memory. It was a moment before she realized that she was back in her room at Christy and Zachary's place, a moment more before she heard deep and even breathing.

Still, she thought it was only Augustus, but in the glow of lantern light coming in through her door, open just a crack, she saw a man's form sprawled in the room's one chair. She didn't need to see clearly to know it was Webb—her heart told her.

He was safe. Thank God, he was safe.

"Go back to sleep," he grumbled.

Megan pretended to be indignant, though she wasn't sure how well she succeeded, because the truth was, she was glad he was there. Gladder than she'd ever been about anything. "I don't have to take orders from you," she pointed out.

He laughed, then yawned expansively. Megan wished they were already married, so that he could lie beside her on the bed, maybe hold her in his arms. "We'll discuss that later," he said. "Right now, I haven't got the gumption it would take to settle the matter."

"There are other beds in this house," she whispered, because she didn't have the strength for a debate, either. Not at the moment, at any rate. "Why are you sleeping in a chair?"

"I'm not sleeping," he pointed out with some regret. "And I wanted to be close to you. Make sure you didn't go sneaking off to confront the whole Sioux nation or try to haul in a few outlaws for the reward."

She smiled in the darkness. He wanted to be close to her.

He yawned again. "Megan?"

"What?"

"Don't ever scare me like that again. I damn near had a heart attack when I saw you out there, in the middle of a storm, with the whole countryside crawling with outlaws."

She was silent. After all, she couldn't make a promise she wasn't sure she could keep.

"Megan." He was quietly insistent.

"I'll try," she said, with little or no hope of success.

He chuckled again. "I guess that'll have to be good enough, for now anyway."

She swallowed hard, dropped her voice to a whisper. "What about Jesse? Have you seen him?"

"He must have taken to the hills."

"He tried to do the right thing, Webb."

"He was a little late."

"He's your brother."

"Go back to sleep."

She persisted. "Come and lie here with me. You'll never get any rest in that chair."

"I'd never get any rest lying next to you on a bed, either," he replied dryly. "Except maybe the permanent kind, if Zachary, your sister, or Caney came in here and shot me for a rascal."

She closed her eyes, trying to think of something to say, and the next thing she knew, there was light at the window, and the smells of freshly brewed coffee and frying bacon filled the air. The chair beside the bedroom door was empty, and Megan wondered if she'd only dreamed that Webb had returned, had sat there keeping watch over her well into the night. Suppose he hadn't come back at all but instead lay trampled or shot, somewhere in the canyon?

She hastened out of bed and into a practical brown cotton dress either Caney or Christy must have laid out for her to wear. She swallowed her pride and put it on; the garment fit loosely across her breasts, since Christy had a more womanly figure, but just then fashion was about the last thing on Megan's mind.

She wrenched on her stockings and shoes, did what she could with her hair—which wasn't a great deal, given that it was still damp from her flight through the rain the night before—and dashed out into the kitchen.

Christy was there, along with Joseph and little Margaret, who were tucking into their breakfasts with uncommon relish. No doubt they were eager to go outside into the sunshine after being confined to the house for several days by the dismal weather.

Megan opened her mouth to ask about Webb, but Christy answered before she could get the words out.

"He's fine," she said. "So is Zachary. Right now, they're trying to round up what's left of the herd."

"What about the rustlers?" Megan asked. She thought of Jesse again and wondered what would happen to him.

"They got most of them last night. Six of them are in jail."

"Zachary and Webb arrested *six men* by themselves?"

Christy poured coffee and set it down on the table, indicating that Megan ought to take a seat. "Jake and Trace were there, too, along with Mr. Hicks and Gus and several other men from town."

Even after the scene with Webb the night before, there on the hillside, Megan found herself wanting to ride out and find him, make sure he was unhurt. It made no sense, thinking that she could protect him, but there it was. The drive to be near him was deeper than anything she'd ever felt before.

"What are we going to do?" she asked in a small voice.

Christy smiled gently. "Do? Why, we're going to head over to Skye's place, just like we planned, and start stitching up your wedding dress. We all went to town for the silk right after we left you yesterday."

"It's dangerous, caring for a man——"

Christy came to stand beside Megan's chair and laid a hand on her shoulder. "Take my advice," she said.

"Think about the wedding. It's a lot better than fretting."

Megan nodded, but only after she'd weighed her sister's counsel.

"Where's Caney?" Joseph wanted to know. "She don't burn the bacon."

"Doesn't," Christy corrected. Megan noticed her sister didn't defend her own cooking skills. "And Caney's busy. She's going on a trip."

Joseph narrowed his eyes. "Where?"

"Young man," Christy sighed, "there are times when I wish you weren't quite so precocious. Finish your breakfast." She rounded the table, ruffled his hair. "We're going to Aunt Skye's house, and we mustn't be late, because there is a great deal to be done."

Joseph's eyes widened. "Will Hank be there?"

"I would imagine he'll be at school," Christy said. Her expression was tender, though her voice was firm. She knew Joseph would be mightily disappointed if he didn't get to see his cousins before the day was out.

"I want to go to school," he said.

"I thought you wanted to be a deputy instead," Christy replied. Margaret was waving her spoon back and forth over her head, and Christy reached out and gently stayed the small, plump hand. It touched Megan deeply, watching her sister with her children; Christy was a good mother, as Megan had always known she would be.

"Changed my mind," Joseph said seriously. "Deputies have to work outside all night, in the rain. Pa told me so this morning." He might have been a miniature man, the way he spoke, instead of a child not yet three years old. If he was that smart at his tender age, Megan reflected, Christy and Zachary would have their hands full bringing him up.

Christy patiently wiped Margaret's hand clean with a checkered table napkin, then gave her back the spoon. Over the heads of her children, Christy met Megan's gaze and smiled. Plainly, for all the uncertainties in her life, she was completely happy. Furthermore, she seemed to have every confidence that Megan would be, too.

The house Skye and Jake shared with their young family was much smaller than the mansion Jake had owned in town before the fire swept through and burned the place to the ground, but it was still impressive. The walls were white clapboard, and there were green shutters at the windows. Crimson roses grew on either side of the flagstone steps leading up onto the spacious veranda, and there were two gables on the second floor. The place's resemblance to Granddaddy McQuarry's Virginia farmhouse filled Megan with a bittersweet sense of nostalgia.

She and Christy had walked the short distance from Christy's, Megan carrying Margaret while Joseph and Augustus tagged along behind.

Skye came out onto the porch, her brown hair swept up into a loose chignon, her smile bright with pleasure at the prospect of company. She was holding little Susannah in her arms. "Where's Bridget?" she asked.

"She'll be along," Christy said.

"And Caney? Is she coming, too?"

Christy and Megan exchanged a look. This was no

time or place to tell their sister the bad news, they tacitly agreed. It was a special day, and there was no reason to spoil it.

"She's busy," Joseph said. Fortunately, he didn't add that Caney was going on a trip. Hank had come through the open doorway, behind Skye, grinning in welcome.

"No school today?" Christy asked, raising an eyebrow.

Skye smiled, somewhat mysteriously. "The latest schoolteacher ran off last week. Married a peddler." Schoolmarms came and went like good weather in Primrose Creek. As soon as they got there, some man was sure to start courting them, there being a shortage of marriageable ladies, and it didn't matter a whit whether they were pretty or homely as a bald chicken.

"What are you going to do?" Christy asked, concerned.

"Go fishing," Hank replied happily, before Skye could answer, and all of them laughed.

The inside of Skye's house proved to be as appealing as the outside, its shiny wooden floors scattered with bright braided rugs, its furniture store-bought. The curtains were of pristine white lace, and a large, splendid oil portrait of Skye hung over the parlor fireplace. She looked like a member of high society, depicted in ropes of pearls and a gauzy rose-colored dress with lots of ruffles and lace.

Following Megan's gaze, Skye blushed prettily. "Jake commissioned that," she said. "I told him it was a foolish extravagance, but he insisted. The last thing I have time to be doing is sitting around all gussied up while somebody paints my picture, but he brought a man all the way from San Francisco to do just that."

"Yes," Christy said, taking off Margaret's cloak and bonnet before attending to her own. "And that fellow stole our *last* schoolteacher."

"Maybe you ought to hire a man," Megan suggested. Skye and Christy both laughed, though she'd been serious.

Within the hour, Bridget arrived with her tribe of children, and soon the older cousins were chasing around outside in the high, fragrant grass, while the little ones played quietly on the floor near Skye's grand dining room table. Megan was measured, fitted, and measured again, but over the course of the morning, the wedding dress began to come together, and, by midafternoon, it was finished except for the lace trim and the pearls. Bridget would add the former, taking the gown home with her that evening, and Christy the latter, after collecting it from Bridget in the morning.

Megan and Christy walked back, Megan once again carrying Margaret, while Joseph pretended to be leading them all safely through the wilderness. When they arrived, the lanterns were lit, and Zachary was there. Plainly exhausted but freshly bathed and shaved, he was at the cookstove, stirring a huge skillet full of hash.

"Supper's about ready," he said with one of his patented grins. "How's the wedding dress coming along?"

Megan glanced around, looking for Caney, knowing already that she wouldn't find her. Christy had made the same deduction, judging by the look in her eyes, but, surely for the children's sake, she made no mention of this noticeable absence.

"Nicely," Christy said, barely missing a beat. "Megan's going to be the prettiest bride this side of Paris."

He'd set the table. He was an unusual man, Zachary was, but then, so were Trace and Jake. Although he nodded, the glow in his eyes was strictly for Christy, and a glance at her flushed sister convinced Megan that the message was getting through, whatever it was. She wondered if she and Webb would ever have a relationship half as deep and gratifying as the one these two shared.

Megan wasn't going to ask about Caney, at least not in front of her niece and nephew, but she had no such compunction where Webb was concerned. She opened her mouth to speak, and before she got the question out, he strolled in from a back room, where he'd evidently washed, shaved, and changed clothes. Although he looked weary, and even a bit gaunt, he had clearly come through the ordeal unscathed, at least physically.

"Zachary invited me to stay for supper," he said.

Once again, Megan felt that humbling urge to run into his arms. It was getting familiar, that feeling, and so were some others that were much more difficult to define. "The cattle?"

He sighed. "We lost twenty head," he said.

She remembered Jesse and felt guilty for not thinking of him first.

Webb didn't wait for her to ask; he'd seen her next question in her eyes. "Jesse's running scared right now," he said, "but I reckon he'll be back one of these days. He's not a bad kid."

Megan might not have understood Webb's loyalty to

his brother if she hadn't had three sisters she would have loved no matter what. "You're not going looking for him?"

"No time," Webb said with obvious regret. "I've got my hands full with only three ranch hands to ride herd."

"Not all the men were in league with the thieves, then," Megan remarked.

"No," Webb agreed. "Not all."

They ate companionably, a family gathered for an ordinary meal, and afterward, when Webb rode home, Megan went with him, sharing his horse, sheltered in the curve of his strong arms, while Augustus ambled along beside them.

Webb didn't speak to her all during the ride home, but Megan wasn't troubled by that, because she knew he was thinking about Jesse. When they arrived at the ranch, he sent her into the house while he went to the barn to groom the horse he'd been riding and saddle a fresh one. Without saying good-bye, he left again, headed for the canyon and what remained of his herd, and Megan watched from the doorway until he was out of sight.

Chapter

9

*W*ebb was chilled, bone-weary, and about halfway discouraged as he rode through the evening wind, headed for the piece of range land where what remained of his herd was grazing. The sky was starless, a great, dark void, but there was a crescent moon and the rain had moved on. God knew they needed all the moisture they could get, but he was glad for the respite all the same.

His mind, meanwhile, kept straying back to the ranch house, back to Megan. He envisioned her moving from room to room, perhaps making tea at the stove, or searching the shelves for a book in the parlor, or maybe getting ready for bed. He found himself lingering on the last possibility; he couldn't help remembering the night before, when she'd so innocently asked him to lie down beside her.

He'd have given just about anything if he could have squared that with himself and accepted the invitation, but his sense of honor had gotten in the way. He'd developed a lot of self-control over the years, but not enough to stretch out on a mattress beside Megan McQuarry without touching her.

He adjusted his hat and sighed. In a few days, they'd be married, he and Megan. He could wait that long. Couldn't he? He was still debating that with himself when he broke through to a small clearing and a rider came out of the trees on the other side. Startled out of some very private thoughts, he automatically reached for the pistol he hadn't carried in better than seven years.

"Webb!" Jesse reined in that broken-down cow pony of his in a thin wash of moonlight, standing in his stirrups.

Webb was at once overjoyed to see the kid and hot to wring his neck. Which only went to show that he hadn't really changed, even though he'd long since hung up his gun. He rode to the middle of the clearing and waited without a word. Jesse had come looking for him, and it was Jesse's place to speak first.

The kid flashed a nervous smile, but he didn't come any closer. Webb estimated the distance between them at fifty yards or so. "I guess you heard I was the one who told Megan them men was planning to steal your cattle," he said. His voice had a shaky quality, though he was trying to sound as though he thought he deserved some credit.

"I don't suppose it occurred to you to tell *me*," Webb observed.

Jesse's horse was fitful, but he kept the reins short. He didn't retreat, but he didn't come any closer, either. "I'm heading back up to Montana," he said. His tone still had a bluff quality. "I stay around here, I'll either be hanged or shot."

Webb understood his worries. Zachary hadn't said what twists and turns the law might take in a case like this one, and even though six of the rustlers Webb had hired on his brother's recommendation were in jail awaiting a military escort to Fort Grant, there were still three of them on the loose. One or all of them might come gunning for Jesse, just on general principle. "I reckon you should have thought of that before."

"Ain't you going to ask why I did it?"

Webb would have smiled under other circumstances. "No," he answered, "I figure I already know. Things were hard for you after I left the Southern Star, weren't they, Jesse? Without me there to take your part, Pa and Tom Jr. must have given you a pretty hard time."

Even at that distance, Webb saw Jesse's face contort with emotion. The boy said nothing, but as Webb rode closer, he noticed that Jesse's breathing was quick and shallow, and his eyes were overly bright.

Soon, they were facing each other like jousting knights on the field of battle, their horses side by side. Webb reached out with his left arm and took the back of Jesse's neck in an affectionate hold. "I shouldn't have left you behind," he said. "I'm sorry."

"You thought you'd killed Tom Jr.," Jesse said, and when Webb let go of him, he looked the other way for a few moments and sniffled.

"Yeah," Webb said. "I surely did. You want to know the worst thing of all? That's exactly what I meant to do. When I went at him that day, I *wanted* to kill him."

"You aren't the only one who ever felt that way," Jesse allowed.

"You sure you want to go back to him and Pa, after being out on your own?"

Jesse thrust out a hard breath, sniffled again, and ran his shirtsleeve across his face. It softened Webb, that gesture; he'd seen his kid brother do that often, when he was a little fella, trying not to cry. "I got to go back," he said with considerable resolution. "At least long enough to prove them wrong about me. I've got some things to prove to myself, too."

If he'd had the time and the leisure, Webb might have done the same thing. "Watch your back," he said. "And send me a telegram when you get as far as Butte."

"You ain't vexed with me?"

Webb nearly smiled. "I didn't say that," he replied. "Given what I did to Tom Jr., I guess it makes sense that you'd want to step lightly around me. I've changed a little since those days, though, Jesse. I've had enough years to wonder what kind of man has that kind of violence in him."

Jesse put out his hand. "Anything you want me to tell Pa?"

The brothers clasped hands for a moment. "Yeah," Webb said. "You can tell the old coot that if I never see him again, it'll be a week too soon. Same goes for Tom Jr."

"What about Ellie?"

Webb grinned. "You tell her I'm happy," he said, "and I wish her the same."

At long last, some light came into Jesse's face. "That Megan, she's going to make you a fine wife."

Webb nodded. "Good-bye, Jesse," he said. "If you want to head back this way, when things have had time to cool down a little, there's a place in the bunkhouse for you."

"Thanks," Jesse said. Then he reined his horse around and rode off, disappearing into the trees on the opposite side of the clearing.

Webb's mind was on the long ago and far away as he rode on toward the herd, but only briefly. The past had no more meaning for him; he'd broken free of it a long while ago, without consciously realizing that, and now that Megan McQuarry was a part of his life, he was only interested in the present and the future.

Megan was wide awake before dawn and determined not to pass another night with chickens in her kitchen. After feeding herself, Augustus, and the chicks—all but three of which had survived—she carried the crate out into the barn and set it on a bale of hay while she fed the horses, taking time to visit a bit with each one of them, the way she would have done with a neighbor.

When the sun was up, she inspected the chicken coop from the inside. The walls were up, and there was even a latch on the door, but only about a third of the roof boards had been nailed into place. Another spate of rainy weather like they'd just had, and the whole project would be ruined.

Shaking her head, Megan found a ladder, a hammer, and some nails in the barn, beside the salvaged lumber Webb had set aside for the purpose. Far from new, the wood was silver-gray with wear from years of sun and wind, rain and snow. The lengths were uneven, too, but for the time being, Megan was only concerned with providing proper shelter for the chicks. If the coop looked too strange when she was finished, she would simply climb up again and saw off the ends.

It was hot work, roofing a chicken coop, and far more difficult in skirts than it would have been in trousers. Nonetheless, Megan spent the morning clambering up and down the ladder, nailing boards in place, getting slivers in her knees. She was finished and sitting on the ridge of the roof, lamenting the gaps where the warped planks didn't fit together, when she got to daydreaming about Webb Stratton and what it would be like to give herself to him, come their wedding night.

As if she'd conjured him, Webb appeared, riding along the creek's edge.

Startled, as chagrined as if he could see into her mind and read her thoughts, she lost her balance and slid straight down one side of the roof on her backside. Unable to catch herself, she scooted right off into midair and fell to the ground with a plunk.

Fortunately, she had not broken her tail bone. *Unfortunately,* her buttocks and the backs of her thighs were prickly with splinters.

Webb reached the yard and, having seen the spectacle, dismounted and sprinted toward her. "Are you hurt?" he demanded. "Good God, you could have broken your neck—"

Megan's eyes filled with tears of humiliation and pain. "I'm hurt," she said.

Instantly, he crouched beside her. "Where? How?"

She scraped her upper lip with her teeth. She didn't want to tell him, but she had to, because this was one problem she couldn't solve by herself. "My—the place where I sit—slivers—"

Although a smile lurked in his eyes, he kept a suitably serious expression. "Now, that," he said, "is a shame." Gently, he helped her to her feet. "Come on. I'd better start pulling."

Megan balked, even though she felt as though she'd sat herself down in an ants' nest. "You could go for Skye, or Christy, or Bridget—"

"And leave you with pieces of wood festering in your hide? Not likely."

Megan simply didn't have the strength to protest further; the only thing greater than her embarrassment was the stinging in her flesh. Augustus accompanied them into the house, whining in sympathy all the while. Megan felt a little like whining herself, but she managed to refrain.

"Let me have a look," Webb said, closing the door.

Megan's face flamed. Try though she might, she could not think of a way out of this dilemma. "This is dreadful," she said, sounding a little like Augustus.

Webb, on the other hand, was all business. "Lift up your skirts," he said.

Utterly abashed, Megan did as she was told. Webb crouched behind her and very carefully lowered her drawers. His only comment on the state of her posterior was a low whistle.

"Is it bad?" Megan dared to inquire. Surely this situation could not get worse.

She was wrong, as it turned out. "Depends on your perspective," he said. "Bend over the table, so I can see."

"I most certainly will not!"

"Megan, you've got more splinters in your backside than I've got cattle. Some of them are in delicate places. Now, do as I tell you, and let's get this over with."

Blushing quite literally from head to foot, Megan leaned over the table, her eyes squeezed tightly shut. In addition to the slivers, and a not inconsiderable breeze, she felt Webb's gently probing fingers, and the sensations *that* produced would probably cause her to find religion.

"You wouldn't—you wouldn't tell anyone about this, would you?" Megan asked, flinching as Webb extracted a particularly stubborn bit of wood.

He chuckled. "Now, who would I tell? I gotta say, though, after this, we might as well already be married."

Megan's face couldn't have been hotter if she'd dipped it in kerosene and lit it with a match. "Perhaps you think this is funny, Mr. Stratton, but I don't!"

Again, that low, brief laugh. "I don't imagine you do," he said. "And, now that you mention it, I *do* think it's funny."

"That is reprehensible!"

"Nonetheless—"

"Are you trying to make this worse?"

"Nope," he said reasonably. "I just figure one of us ought to enjoy it."

Megan considered kicking him, the way a horse might do, and decided against the idea. After all, who knew how many slivers were still protruding from her backside like quills from a porcupine, and she didn't relish the idea of trooping miles along the creek bank, knocking on Skye's door, and starting the whole process over again. "None of this would have happened," she said, "if you'd finished putting the roof on the chicken coop."

"I reckon that's true," he said, with no discernible guilt.

Augustus raised his paws onto the table's edge across from Megan and made a low and mournful sound in his throat. "Your master has no sense of delicacy," she said.

"At least," Webb observed, from behind and below, "his master has the wits not to slide down the roof of a chicken coop on his hind end."

Megan reconsidered kicking him and decided against it again, fearing that he might retaliate in some way. "Can't you hurry?"

"Yes," he answered, "I guess I could. But I might miss a few of these little devils if I did."

In time—roughly the life span of a biblical patriarch, by Megan's calculations—Webb announced that he'd gotten the last of the splinters, and she was ready to rejoice, not to mention right her clothes, when he stopped her. "Not so fast, darlin'," he said. "I still have to paint you with iodine. Otherwise, you might get an infection."

"Iodine!" The word shot out of Megan's mouth like a bullet. "That burns!"

"Yep," Webb agreed. "It'll dye your backside orange, too."

"Oh, thank you."

He had the gall to pat her right on her bare bottom. While she was still fuming, he rose and went to a shelf near the stove for a small medical aid kit containing bandages and the like. When Megan pressed her palms to the tabletop to hoist herself upright, he shook his head. "Don't," he warned. "If you pull up your drawers, I'll just have to pull them down again."

Megan was certainly no prude—she'd spent much of her life on a farm, after all—but that statement disconcerted her so much that she thought she'd choke on her tongue. Webb merely went back to his previous enterprise, this time dabbing on iodine. Every touch of the stuff stung like fire, and there must have been a hundred places where the skin was broken. Finally, finally, it was over.

Webb eased her drawers up over her knees and hips, then lowered her skirts. "You'll want to be careful about sitting down for a while," he said.

Megan would not, *could not,* look at him. Instead, she headed for the stove and started the process of brewing tea.

"If I were in your position," Webb said from near the fireplace, "I'd want whiskey."

"Well," Megan replied sharply, still refusing to meet his gaze, "you're not, more's the pity."

"You know, I must have missed it when you thanked me."

Megan's backbone stiffened like a ramrod. *"Thank* you," she said acidly. She supposed she should be grateful for what he'd done, but she had yet to achieve that noble state of mind.

Suddenly, he was behind her again, but this time

was very different. He stood close and slipped his arms loosely around her waist. "I'm sorry," he said quietly, and with a touch of amusement lingering in his tone. "I shouldn't have teased you. You were real brave."

The way he was holding her was somehow far more intimate than the sliver pulling had been, and instead of resisting, she longed to lean back against him, and that made her furious with herself. She tried to answer—even then, she wasn't sure what she would say—but it was as though her tongue had swollen to fill her mouth. It simply refused to work.

He turned her gently around, raised her chin to look into her face. His smile was tender, his eyes alight with a weary joy. He kissed her forehead, and it seemed to Megan that all of time and creation came to a halt, that she and Webb were somehow outside both, in a realm all their own.

Webb was the first to speak. "I've got to get back to the herd," he said presently, with great reluctance.

Megan nodded. He wasn't even gone yet, and already she missed him. Which seemed incredible, given that only minutes before, she'd considered planting one heel in the middle of his face.

He started to move away, then stayed. "Megan—" He paused, started again. "About the wedding—how long do we have to wait?"

Megan could only gape at him for a long moment. Then, careful not to trip over her tongue, she asked, "Wait?"

He smiled, traced the length of her nose with the tip of one index finger. "Yes," he said. "I figure this Saturday would be good. Agreed?"

Saturday. She was going to be Webb Stratton's wife in just a few days. It seemed too good to be true. "Saturday," she agreed with a shy nod.

He leaned down and kissed her mouth in a leisurely way that left her trembling inside. Then, eyes smiling again, he said, "Stay off the roof of the chicken coop."

She laughed and whacked his chest with the heels of both palms.

A few minutes later, he'd ridden away, and she and Augustus went outside to reclaim the crate of chicks from the barn and settle them inside the new coop. After spreading straw on the dirt floor of the little hut and setting out feed and water, she set the birds free in their new home. Augustus was waiting on the other side of the chicken house door when she came out, and he greeted her as eagerly as if she'd been away for days.

As she walked back toward the empty house, however, loneliness filled her in much the same way twilight was filling the high valley. She missed Webb, of course, but the loss of Caney was just coming home to her, and she ached with the knowledge that she might never see her good friend again. When she was married on Saturday, Caney would not be there with the rest of the family, and that was hard to imagine, though she understood how hard such an occasion might be for the other woman.

If only Mr. Hicks would come to his senses, go after Caney, and bring her home.

"Miss Caney Blue!"

Caney, riding through the woods on a mule borrowed from Trace Qualtrough, recognized the voice, and she tried to pick up the pace.

"Woman," Malcolm Hicks said, drawing alongside her on one of Jake Vigil's fancy horses, "I am talkin' to you."

"You ain't got nothin' to say that I want to hear," Caney answered. That wasn't true, of course, but she was through hoping for things that weren't going to happen. For the past several years, she'd cooked and sewed for Mr. Hicks. She'd walked with him and let him hold her hand, and when he was down sick after the big fire, from breathing smoke, she'd looked after him for a solid week, with the whole town gossiping. And in all that time, whenever she brought up the possibility of holy matrimony, he'd found some way to distract her.

He reached down and grabbed hold of the mule's bridle. He was a handsome man, with sleek bright skin, dark as a night sky, and the kindest pair of eyes Caney had ever looked into. He was broad in the shoulders and strong as the horse he rode, and just looking at him made Caney feel weak all through, even now, when she'd made up her mind not to have a thing to do with the no'count rascal ever again.

"You can't go leavin'," he said.

"You just hide and watch," Caney spat back. If she didn't act tough, she was going to break down and cry like a baby. The only thing she'd ever really wanted in all her life, besides a red petticoat with black satin bows stitched to the ruffles, was this one cussed man, and he didn't want to be married.

"I love you," he told her earnestly, and by the way

his brow was furrowed, she thought he might mean it.

She was so stunned, she couldn't find a thing to say.

"I said I love you," he repeated in a louder voice, apparently under the impression that she hadn't heard him the first time.

"Talkin' is easy," she managed. "It's *doin'* that signifies."

He thrust out an enormous sigh. "If you don't want to stay and marry me, I can't force you to do it. I'm a poor man, Caney Blue. I can't give you much besides a little company house over by the lumber yard and my name. A woman like you deserves a whole lot more."

"Maybe I do," Caney said softly, her eyes prickling with tears, "but all I want, Malcolm Hicks, is to be your missus, right and proper."

"Then come back with me. Reverend Taylor will marry us up tonight."

Caney's heart soared. She would have Mr. Hicks for her own after all, and maybe some babies, too. "What took you so long, Malcolm?" she asked, right there in the middle of noplace, sitting astride a mule.

He averted his gaze, looked back. "I had a wife once. I told you that." His eyes were wet, but he didn't seem shamed by it. He didn't even try to wipe his face. "Becky and me, we was slaves on the same place. She was carryin' when the *master* decided she was distractin' me from my work and ought to be sold. Sold." He stopped, and a great shudder went through him. "He sent her away, and I never did find her again, though I tried. The good Lord knows I tried." He fell silent again, and memories contorted his fine, proud face. "Then, just before I came here to work for Jake Vigil, I met up with a feller I knew back in Georgia. We worked in the fields together. And he told me my Becky had died in that new place, having our child."

Caney was too stricken to weep. She managed to put out a tentative hand, touch Malcolm's arm. "I'm so sorry," she said.

Malcolm shook his head, caught up in memories. "I swore I'd never let myself care for any woman again the way I cared for Becky. It just hurt too much."

"What happened to the child?" Caney asked. She knew it was a painful question, and none of her affair into the bargain, but she had to know.

"That's the worst part," Malcolm said. "I never did hear. That baby would be ten years old now if it lived. I got to spend the rest of my life wonderin'—wonderin' if I got a son or a daughter. Wonderin' if my child's got food in his belly, a place to lay his head. And I ain't never gonna know for sure."

Caney reached up, touched his cheek tenderly. Now her face was as wet as his. "You just listen here to me, Malcolm Hicks. You *is* going to be wonderin', but I'll be right there wonderin' with you, if that counts for anything."

He leaned down until his forehead touched against hers. "Don't you leave me, Caney. Don't you *ever* leave me."

Caney vowed that she wouldn't, and two hours later, when she and Malcolm stood in front of Reverend Taylor exchanging their vows, she made the same promises all over again, in different words, though it wouldn't have been necessary. Once Caney

Blue gave her word, it was solid as a mountain and didn't need giving a second time.

She'd never been happier in her life, not even with Titus, the husband she'd liked and respected but never quite loved. All the same, it stuck in her mind, her conversation with Malcolm. It was a fearful trial to be left wondering about lost kin—Malcolm had suffered for a long time. And so, because of her, had Bridget and Christy, Skye and Megan, her girls. She'd finally broken down and told Skye and Megan about their poor mama, but Bridget and Christy didn't know where they came from, except that they'd both had Thayer McQuarry for a papa. She wondered if they were strong enough to hear the truth.

Gus arrived in the morning, quite unexpectedly, with a loaded wagon and a broad grin. Megan went out to greet him, waiting while he drove the rig across a shallow place in the creek. Augustus ran up and down the bank, barking with elation, and it seemed to Megan that she was perfectly happy in that moment beside the sun-dazzled stream. She was going to marry Webb. She had a family and friends, with and without fur, and she would live out the rest of her life on the land her granddaddy had left to her. A person couldn't ask for more without being downright greedy.

"What have you brought?" she demanded good-naturedly, smiling and shading her eyes with one hand.

"I bring wedding present," Gus called down, his round face filled with delight. He loved being the bearer of glad tidings.

The wagon bed was covered with a canvas tarp, and

Megan was more than curious. Whatever Gus had brought, it was big, and it was bulky.

"Is gift from Diamond Lil," he added when Megan didn't ask.

The reminder of Lil Colefield and the agreement they'd made took some of the starch out of Megan; with all that had happened, she'd forgotten her promise to help get the show house started. She had given her word lightly, and now she would have to keep it. No longer smiling, Megan lifted a corner of the tarp and peeped underneath, but all she could see was a finely carved section of wood.

"Is bed," Gus said. "I bring mattress in afternoon."

Megan's face warmed a little, but after bending over a table for half an hour while Webb pried out slivers, it took more to embarrass her. "Diamond Lil sent us a *bed*?"

Gus didn't reply directly, probably because the answer was lying right there in the back of his wagon for all the world to see. He tossed back the tarp to reveal a beautiful bed frame of carved mahogany, with four pineapple posts. It would have to be assembled, but Gus had brought his tool box along, no doubt for that very purpose.

"You show me where to put," he said.

Megan had been in Webb's room upstairs, though only to make the bed and sweep, of course, and she'd seen the cot he slept on. Obviously, that would not do for a married couple. She turned to lead the way and to hide the added heat that had climbed her neck to glow in her cheeks. She wondered what Webb would have to say about such a gift and how he'd react when she told him about her unofficial partnership with Lil.

Gus was bull-strong, and after he'd surveyed the master bedroom and they had decided that the frame ought to go between the two big windows opposite the fireplace, he carried in the gigantic piece of furniture, piece by piece, and assembled it. Watching from the doorway, Megan couldn't help anticipating her first night in this room, as Webb's wife, and all those that would follow. Whatever problems they might face, and surely they would have their share, here was their sanctuary, the heart of the house, where they would talk, sharing their hopes, dreams, and fears, or *not* talk, on those inevitable nights when they were fractious with each other or simply too tired to string words together into sensible sentences.

"It's beautiful," she said when Gus had finished. She would ride to town, as soon as she could, and thank Diamond Lil for the gift in person. She probably should not have accepted something so expensive and so personal in the first place, but she didn't have the heart to disappoint Gus that way, let alone Lil Colefield. "Thank you, Gus."

She offered him coffee after that, but he refused politely, saying he had to get back to the store. He would bring the mattress, he reiterated, sometime in the afternoon.

He was as good as his word, arriving several hours later with the promised item, and he was still seated at the table, enjoying coffee and plum cake, when Webb showed up, dirty from the trail but otherwise in good spirits. The closer Saturday came, Megan had noticed with some satisfaction, the more cheerful he became.

"Hullo, Gus," he said, pleased, offering his hand after hanging up his hat. "What brings you out here?"

Before Gus could answer, Megan did. "Gus brought us a bedstead. It was a gift from Diamond Lil." She couldn't wait to ask her future husband how the saloon owner and madam of a notorious brothel had known he didn't own a proper bed, and she saw by the faint flush in Webb's tanned face that he was dreading the question.

His discomfort amused her a little, partly because of the sliver episode and partly because, when she finally told him about her promise to Lil, she wouldn't be the only one with some explaining to do. "Well, now," he said, and rubbed the back of his neck. That was all, just "Well, now."

In good time, after inspecting the chickens, who were sprouting real feathers and growing at an astounding rate, and talking horses with Webb for a while out in the barn, Gus finally climbed back into his wagon and headed home.

Webb came into the house, carried a basin of water out onto the kitchen step, took off his shirt, and began to wash himself industriously. The splashes beaded in his hair and on his skin, glittering with fragments of refracted sunlight.

"What prompted Diamond Lil to give us a bed?" he asked, drying himself with the towel Megan provided.

"I was going to ask you that very thing, Mr. Stratton," she replied.

"I might have said something," he admitted.

"To Lil?" Megan inquired lightly.

He shook his head, thrust a hand through his damp hair. "One of the girls. They gossip just like all females." He paused, sighed, rested his hands on his hips. The gesture, usually an indication of stubbornness, seemed almost defensive. "Megan, I won't deny that I've spent time upstairs at Lil's. A man gets real lonely out here without a wife. But I won't be going back there, ever—I give you my word on that."

She hid a smile. "Not even to the saloon?"

He grinned. "I didn't say that," he pointed out.

Her turn. She drew in a deep breath, let it out slowly. "Lil is building a show house," she blurted out, just to get it over with. "She asked me to be a silent partner and help her get started, and I said I would."

Webb's face was unreadable, but he wasn't smiling, and that wasn't a good sign. "You're going to be an actress again?" he asked. He'd brought one foot to rest on the top step, and now he leaned, both arms folded, against his raised knee. "Seems to me that won't leave you much time to be a wife and mother."

Dread rose within Megan, but she did a good job of hiding it. Or, at least, she thought she did. "There might come a time when I'm called upon to play a part or two," she admitted, "but mostly I'll just be helping to arrange the entertainments."

"I see," Webb answered, and everything about him indicated just the opposite to be true.

"Webb, I promised," Megan said.

He looked her up and down. "We've made a few promises to each other, you and I," he said, "even if they were unspoken."

"And I'll keep them."

He was quiet for a long time, tilting his head back, looking up at the blue summer sky. When he met Megan's gaze again, he said the one thing that made it impossible for them to agree. "I guess you'll have to make a choice or two before Saturday, won't you?"

"**D**on't be bull-headed," Christy said the following afternoon, when she and Bridget came by to give the wedding dress a final fitting. Megan was standing on a chair in the center of the kitchen, while Bridget knelt, pinning the hem into place, and Christy adjusted the seams. She had just explained her quandary concerning Lil and the new show house, describing her promise and Webb's ultimatum.

Bridget looked up. "Just tell Miss Colefield you made a mistake."

Megan's conscience was giving her as much trouble as the slivers in her backside had done, maybe more, and she expected she'd be a lot longer in the healing if she made the wrong choice. She heaved a frustrated sigh.

"Hold still," Christy scolded, giving her a pinch on one side of her waist to make the point. Her gray eyes were direct and perhaps a little fierce. "What do you really *want* to do, Megan?"

Megan bit her lower lip and willed the tears burning behind her eyes into full retreat. "I want to marry Webb," she said. "I want to live in this house with him until I'm an old, old lady. I want a flock of babies. But a part of me wants what Lil's offering, too."

Bridget tugged hard at the elegant, rustling skirts of the magnificent dress. Between her touches of lace and the dozens of tiny pearls Christy had stitched to the bodice and the cuffs of the full, billowing sleeves, that gown was as fine as any she could have bought in Richmond before the Great Strife. "All of us have to make choices sometimes," she said. "Nobody can do everything."

"Do you have any idea how busy you'll be, once you have children?" Christy argued. "Good heavens, Megan, you're already responsible for cooking meals and cleaning the place, not to mention everything *else* that goes with being a wife. You purely won't have the *time* to do a proper job in either place. And if I know you, you'd wear yourself to a nub trying, all the same."

"He's never said he loved me," Megan confided in a small voice.

Bridget and Christy looked at each other before focusing their gazes on Megan's face. "Have you ever told Webb you love *him?*" Christy asked.

Megan swallowed. "No," she said.

"Why not?" Bridget wanted to know.

Megan sniffled and barely caught herself from touching the back of one hand to her nose. "I'm not sure it would be honest."

They both stopped working. Bridget got to her feet, and Christy stepped back, frowning. "What?" Christy demanded.

"What I mean is," Megan began, wincing once and wringing her hands, "I feel all sorts of things for Webb Stratton, but I don't know if it's love. It's not like anything I've ever felt before."

Again, a cryptic glance passed between the two elder sisters. "What, exactly, *is* it like?" Bridget asked.

Megan felt much the way she had when she'd been bent over the kitchen table with her bare bottom in the air, but she needed Bridget and Christy's help, so she bore it with as much grace as possible. Nonetheless, her face was hot, and there were grasshoppers springing about in her stomach. "Sometimes it's like nothing and nobody else exists, except for Webb and me," she said in a whisper, though the three of them were quite alone, except for Augustus, who was snoozing on the hearth. "I know I can live without him, but I also know it would be a darker, thinner, more hollow life. And when he kisses me—"

Both Bridget and Christy leaned forward, the better to listen.

"When he kisses me," Megan went on, "I always feel as if I'm going to faint. My insides catch fire just like dry timber, and I ache to beat all."

A smile crept across Christy's mouth. "You love him," she said with quiet confidence.

Bridget's cornflower-blue eyes sparkled. "Oh, yes," she agreed. "You most definitely do."

"What do I know?" Megan wailed. "I thought I loved Davy Trent!"

Bridget raised one eyebrow and folded her arms. Obviously, she had no idea who Davy was and what had happened between him and Megan. Just as obviously, she had her suspicions. She didn't ask, though. She just stood there with her usual authority, waiting to be enlightened.

"Did he make you feel the same things Webb does?" Christy asked carefully. "This Davy person, I mean?"

Megan felt as though Christy had just flung a bucket full of dirty mop water all over her, unprovoked. "Of *course* he didn't!" she hissed.

"There you have it," Bridget said solemnly, addressing Christy rather than Megan. The pair had been embattled for much of their lives, and yet they shared an alliance that set them apart from the rest of the family in a subtle and unique way. "Webb is the one for her."

"Yes," Christy agreed. "I think you're right."

"Does it matter at all here what *I* think?" Megan cried softly, and Augustus whimpered and got to his feet, as though he thought she might need rescuing.

"What *do* you think?" Christy reiterated.

Megan burst into tears. "I won't be able to bear it," she sobbed, "if he calls off the wedding. It's bad enough that Caney won't be there!"

"The dilemma seems simple enough to me," Bridget said. Sometimes it made a body want to stick pins in her, the way she was always so damnably certain of everything. "Marry him, Megan. What does the Good Book say? 'It's better to marry than to burn'?" She paused for effect, and Megan remembered that she wasn't the only one in the family with a sense of drama. "If you ask me, you're about to go up in flames right now. As for Caney, she'll come back when she's ready. Just you wait and see."

"You really think so?" Skye asked softly.

Bridget nodded. "We're her family," she said.

Despite Bridget's claim that the matter of Webb's decree was settled, Megan felt like a hound who's just chased a rabbit round and round the same bush for half an hour without catching it. She was as confused as ever; they hadn't settled anything. Still, she was comforted by the prospect of Caney's eventual return.

Christy handed her a dish towel, that being the first thing that came to hand for the purpose. "Here. Dry your face and blow your nose before you ruin that dress," she ordered.

Megan wiped her eyes, but that was as far as she was willing to go. After all, she had to *use* that dish towel. "You two were absolutely no help at all," she accused.

Bridget smiled. "You don't need our help anyhow," she said. "You already know what you have to do."

Megan realized that indeed she *did* know. She was going to have to choose between love and honor, in this case, and she would follow her heart and choose love. She would tell Webb what she'd decided, as humbling as that would be, then go to town and make her apologies to Diamond Lil. No doubt the saloon mistress would want her four-poster pineapple bedstead back.

She nodded. "You're right," she said. "Both of you. Jupiter and Zeus, I hate that."

Christy and Bridget laughed out loud, their voices as beautiful as distant bells on a Sunday morning, and returned to the task at hand.

*   *   *

He'd been unreasonable, Webb thought, saddle-sore and sick to death of looking at cows and cowboys. Sure, it was unusual for a married woman to be in business, but Megan was no ordinary female. That was one of the many reasons he loved her.

He sighed. Yep, he loved her. What he'd felt for Ellie had been mere infatuation; he'd known that for a long time. It was Megan he wanted to share his life with, Megan he wanted to bear his children, Megan he wanted to lie down beside, every night until he died. Still, he was a proud man, and it would be a bitter pill, having his wife go into business with the town madam. Sweet heaven, he'd be joshed damn near to death over that, and he might even have to take up fighting again.

"Rider!" the lookout—one of Jake Vigil's lumber-jacks, borrowed until more men could be hired—shouted to Webb, pointing up the ravine.

Webb lifted his gaze and knew immediately that the visitor was Megan. He spurred the gelding into a trot and headed straight uphill.

He and Megan met midway.

"Webb—" she began.

"Megan—" he started.

They laughed. "You go first," Webb said. It was good just to look at her, just to hear her voice. A home-coming of sorts.

"No," she said. "You."

He sighed, the reins lying easy in his gloved hands, which rested on the pommel of his saddle. "I still hate the idea of your working in town," he said. "It's going to look like I can't provide for my own wife, and God knows what the gossips will say. All the same, I had no right forcing you to choose." He paused, searched the horizon for inspiration, and looked back at her. "What it comes down to is, I'll take you any way I can get you."

She blushed prettily, and joy shone in her eyes. "Webb," she said, in a tone so tender that it had the effect of a caress. Then she shook her head. "I won't be working with Lil, not unless she runs into a real emergency," she said. "Part of this ranch will be mine, and that will be more than enough to keep me busy, when you figure in a husband and babies."

Something leaped inside him. He almost said it then, almost said right out that he loved her. It didn't seem like the proper place to make such a declaration, though, there in the middle of noplace, with cows and a few saddle bums for witnesses. His voice came out hoarse. "I'm for starting that first baby as soon as possible," he said.

She went even pinker, but the tears were gone, and her eyes were still shining. "That's something we can agree on. Will you be home for supper tonight?"

Webb knew he shouldn't leave the herd. He was short-handed as it was, and the weather was still uncertain. If he lost any more cattle, he'd have a problem, and not a slight one. "I'll be there," he heard himself say.

His reward was a smile, that sweet, sassy Megan McQuarry smile that always made his gizzard shimmy up into his windpipe. "I'll be waiting," she said.

Lordy, he thought, and sat there in the saddle like a lump on a log, watching her ride away.

When, resigned, he reined his horse around to go back to work, he saw Trace and Zachary coming toward him on horseback, with Jake Vigil and Malcolm Hicks close behind.

When they got within shouting distance, he saw that Trace and Zachary were grinning from ear to ear. Damn pleased with themselves.

"Figured you could use some more help with these dogies," Zachary said, indicating the cattle with a toss of his head.

Webb was at a loss for words. He'd been on his own a long time, even before he'd left the Southern Star, in many ways, and now he was going to have brothers, the kind a man could count on in good times and bad.

"You do want some help, don't you?" Trace inquired, still smiling.

"God, yes," Webb said at last.

Jake rode forward, put out a hand. "I hope you appreciate this," he said, his eyes bright with amusement. "Malcolm here got up out of his marriage bed to lend a hand."

Webb had never seen a black man blush, but he reckoned that was what Malcolm did just then. He sure did curse.

"He and Caney got themselves hitched in secret," Zachary said, standing in the stirrups to stretch his legs. "I'll allow that I envy him her cooking."

Malcolm smiled at that. He did look happy, Webb thought. "My missus can spare me for a little while," Hicks said. "But it don't work the other way."

"What we need to do," Webb said, his voice a little

unsteady, "is drive these cattle closer to the house. Now that twenty or so of them are gone for good, the high meadow will serve as grazing land, at least for a few weeks."

"Makes sense," Zachary agreed.

Within half an hour, with four extra hands to help, Webb's herd was on its way up out of the ravine, toward higher ground, and Webb himself was on his way home.

To say walking straight into Diamond Lil's infamous saloon in broad daylight drew stares and whispers would be an understatement, but Megan did so with her shoulders squared and her head held high. She had something to say to the woman, and it had to be said face-to-face.

Just past the swinging doors, Megan paused and waited, blinking, for her eyes to adjust to the dimmer light. She saw a long, narrow room with sawdust-covered floors and high, murky windows. The bar seemed as long as the railroad tracks between New York and Philadelphia, laid out straight as the crow flies, and the mirror behind it must have cost as much as the rest of the building. There were tables with green felt tops, and a few early customers were hunkered over glasses of whiskey, like freezing men trying to absorb the heat of a faltering bonfire. The infamous "girls" who worked upstairs were nowhere to be seen, somewhat to Megan's disappointment.

The bartender stopped wiping the glass in his hands, and his mouth dropped open. "I'll be jiggered," he said.

"I'm looking for Lillian Colefield," Megan said clearly, though her voice was shaking. The McQuarry women had a reputation for boldness, but this was new ground, even for them.

"Well, here I am," Lil said, appearing in a doorway at the back of the room. It looked like three miles, the distance between where Megan stood and that door. "Come on back to my office, and we'll jaw awhile." She took in the staring patrons of the bar. "You fellas just shove your eyeballs back in your heads and go on about your business. Haven't you ever seen a decent woman before?"

Megan might have been walking in knee-deep mud as she made her way through that saloon. If word ever got back to Caney, wherever she was, she'd get a lecture that would blister both her ears. On the other hand, what else could she have done? Stood in the street and yelled for Lil to come out?

Lil's office surprised Megan; she'd expected silk and satin, sumptuous cushions and fainting couches, perhaps, and velvet draperies with tassels. Instead, the place was utterly plain, with just a desk, a couple of chairs, and shelves full of books and ledgers. A little stove stood in the corner.

"Sit down," Lil said, taking her own seat behind the desk and folding her hands loosely. She wasn't dressed like a madam, either, Megan noted. Her dress was brown bombazine, unadorned, and without cosmetics, her face reflected the hard life she'd led. A smile tipped up the corner of her mouth. "What brings you here, Miss McQuarry?"

Not for the first time in her life, Megan wished she

could be two women, one of them Webb's wife and the
mother of his children, the other helping to build the
Primrose Creek Playhouse into something the community would be proud to claim. She sat up very straight
and took the plunge. "I'm afraid I cannot be your partner after all. I'm sorry."

Lil arched one eyebrow. "Webb put his foot down,
did he?"

Megan's face flared, and her backbone lengthened
another notch, as if she'd grown an extra vertebra. "I
made the decision myself," she said firmly. It wasn't
entirely true, of course, but that was beside the point.
"Thank you for the beautiful bed. I suppose you'll be
wanting it back now."

Lil laughed. "You keep the bed," she said. "It's my
gift to the both of you."

Megan didn't know what to say, now that she'd
stated her intentions regarding the partnership. She
hadn't had much experience conversing with brothel
owners, her scandalous career as an actress notwithstanding. "Th-thank you," she faltered, and then realized that she'd repeated herself.

Lil took a cheroot out of a box on her desk and,
before lighting up, offered one to Megan, who refused
with a shake of her head. The older woman sat back
in her chair and regarded her visitor through a haze
of blue-gray smoke. "You've got a good mind and a
lot of gumption. Not many women would walk right
into Diamond Lil's saloon in the middle of the afternoon."

Megan's smile was rueful. "I was an actress. I'm
accustomed to being talked about."

"Are you?" Lil countered quietly. "I never did get used to it, myself."

Megan wanted to ask Lillian Colefield how she'd become Diamond Lil, but it would have been prying, and, like the other McQuarrys, she did her best to confine snooping to members of her own family. She sighed. "It's hard. I'd like to be like them—the 'good women' of Primrose Creek—but I can't seem to get the knack of it."

Lil smiled. "Oh, they'll come around in time, once you're safely settled down. You won't be such a threat to them then."

Megan frowned. "A threat?"

"Yes," Lil drawled, drawing on her cheroot with frank enjoyment and exhaling the smoke in a way that seemed almost elegant. "They look at you, pretty as a flower garden after a long winter, and smart to boot, and they see all the things they'll never have or be. Once you're married, they'll be able to convince themselves that you'll end up just like them, sooner or later. I don't think that will happen, though."

Megan's eyes were wide. "You don't?" she asked in a hopeful voice.

Lil smiled. "You're different. Like the other women in your family. Challenges only make you stronger. Somebody breaks your heart, you'll learn to love more, and better. Your grandfather would have been proud of you."

Megan's breath caught in her throat, fairly choking her. Everything in this woman's tone and bearing implied that she'd known Granddaddy, but that was impossible, wasn't it?

"I was born and raised in Richmond," Lil went on. "I met your grandfather only twice, and not under pleasant circumstances either time, but I could tell he was worth ten of that son of his, charming as my Thayer was. I adored him, even though he did me wrong more than once."

Megan could barely speak. The coattails of an idea flickered at the edge of her thoughts, but she couldn't quite grasp them. "You knew——?"

"Your granddaddy paid me to leave the state of Virginia forever after Christy was born, and I did. He'd come to claim Bridget when she was a week old, and I let her go, too. Thayer was long gone by the time Christy came along—I heard he'd gone to New Orleans, one jump ahead of somebody's husband." Lil paused, and her eyes were fixed on something in the invisible distance. "I knew I couldn't give my babies the kind of life I wanted them to have, not the way I lived, but it was hard to let them go all the same."

Megan closed her eyes. "Why are you telling me this?"

"I've kept my secret for twenty-odd years. I reckon I'm just tired of carrying the load."

"Why did you come here—to Primrose Creek?"

"I knew your granddaddy had a tract of land out here. He'd taken it as security for a debt, I believe. I worked my way west and decided to take a look at the place before heading on to San Francisco. I liked it here, saw the potential, and stayed instead."

"Bridget and Christy are—are you daughters." Megan was still trying to absorb the fact.

"Yes," Lil said. She looked so weary, so beaten

down, in that moment that Megan felt sorry for her. "Imagine my delight when the four of you showed up here."

"Didn't you ever want to tell them? To see them?"

"I do see them, all the time. Primrose Creek is a small town. As for telling them about myself, well, I couldn't quite bring myself to look them in the face and say their mama was a saloon keeper and, once, a whore. Besides, that was what your granddaddy paid me for— to stay out of their lives. In spite of what most folks think of me, I'm not without honor."

Megan felt dizzy. "You're the secret Caney's been keeping all this time," she said.

Lil nodded. "She wasn't pleased when she realized who I was, but she and I weren't entirely in disagreement. She thought, as I did, that my daughters ought to be left to believe what they'd been told all their lives."

Megan rose shakily to her feet. "And now?"

Lil spread her elegant, long-fingered hands. Close up, Megan could see things in her countenance and her appearance that reminded her of both Christy and Bridget—grace, for example, and courage and intelligence as well. "I guess that's up to you," she said.

All too aware of the burden that had been laid on her shoulders, Megan rose shakily to her feet. "You've put me in a fine position," she said. "Do you expect me to explain everything to Christy and Bridget, so you don't have to do it?"

Lil looked sad. "Think what you like," she said.

Megan had no answer for that, no answer for anything. She simply nodded in farewell, turned around, and walked out of the office and straight through the saloon without looking to either side.

She'd been home less than half an hour, still moving in a daze, when Caney showed up, driving one of Jake Vigil's rigs. If she hadn't already been in a state of shock, seeing her dear friend would have done the job.

"You came back!" she cried in relief and delight, standing in the doorway and gripping the framework with one hand. Caney would attend her wedding after all. Maybe she'd even changed her mind about leaving Primrose Creek to start over someplace else.

Caney smiled as she set the wagon brake and climbed down. "Mr. Malcolm Hicks came to his senses, right enough," she said, holding out her left hand to show a narrow gold band. "We got ourselves married. Been honeymoonin' ever since."

Megan shouted for joy, and the two women embraced, but when they went inside, Caney's aspect changed.

"What was you doin' in Diamond Lil's this afternoon?" she demanded, taking Megan by the upper arms.

"You know about that?" Megan asked, and gulped. "A-already?"

"The whole town knows!" Caney snapped. Despite her flaring nostrils and narrowed eyes, Megan realized, Caney wasn't so much angry as frightened. "Place is buzzin' like a hive full of scalded bees. What in the world was you thinkin' of?"

Megan wouldn't have explained herself to anyone else on earth, not even Webb. "I was going to be Lil's partner." At the look on Caney's face, she hurried on.

"She's building a show house. Anyhow, I had to tell her I'd changed my mind."

"That's all?" Caney asked. "That's all that happened?"

Megan couldn't lie, especially not to this woman who had been a second mother to her. "No," she said. "She told me about—about Bridget and Christy."

"Lord have mercy!" Caney gasped, and spread one hand over her heart in such a way that Megan was momentarily terrified for her. "I got to sit myself right down!"

Megan took Caney's arm and ushered her to a chair at the table. Then she brought her a cup of cold water and watched protectively while she sipped. When Caney looked up, her eyes were dark with pain.

"I suppose you plan to tell them."

"I think they ought to know," Megan said quietly. "But I'm not sure it's my place to tell them, or yours, either."

"How you gonna keep a secret like this?" Caney asked anxiously. "It'll chew you up inside."

Megan sat down in the chair next to Caney's and took the other woman's strong hands into her own. "What about you? This must have been a terrible burden for you to carry all these years."

"It wasn't so hard at first. I believed it was best. But now you're grown women, the four of you." She let out a long, shaky sigh. "It's my place to tell them the truth," she said after a brief silence, during which a myriad of emotions crossed her face. "Christy and Bridget deserve to know. It's goin' to throw them some, though."

Megan nodded. "Yes," she said. "But the truth is always better than a lie, isn't it? And they have Trace and Zachary to lean on. Frankly, I think they'll be glad to finally know, once they get over the initial shock."

Caney pulled free and covered her mouth with one hand, clearly fighting back sobs, maybe even hysteria. Her eyes were huge and round, and she looked ashen. "*Glad?*" she mocked, but not unkindly, when she'd gained some control. "To find out they have a whore for a mama?"

Megan stiffened. "Lillian is a lot more than a—a woman of the evening, Caney. She's strong, and she's smart, too. Just look at all she's accomplished." She stopped, remembering the interview in Diamond Lil's plain office, revelation by revelation. "She gave Christy and Bridget to Granddaddy because she wanted them to have a real family and a home."

Caney lowered her eyes, raised them again. They were filled with fire. "We've all had hard times," she said. "And we didn't take to whorin' to put food on the table!"

Megan stroked Caney's cheek, so glad to have her back that she couldn't begin to express what she felt. "Who knows what made her what she is? Maybe she thought Thayer was going to marry her, in the beginning. Maybe she loved him."

Caney laughed and sniffled at the same time. "You suppose they'll forgive me, my Christy and Bridget?"

"I don't think there's anything to forgive," Megan said softly. "We all know you were merely trying to protect us."

Caney rallied significantly after that. "What kind of

manners you got, girl? You ain't even offered me a cup of tea, and here I am, back to stay."

Megan kissed her friend's forehead. "Thank heaven," she said. "I don't know what any of us would do without you."

"Stop your carryin' on," Caney commanded, bluffing, "and make that tea."

Megan lay in her narrow bed in the small spare room downstairs, off the kitchen, staring at the ceiling and thinking of her wedding day. Her splendid dress, carefully pressed and hung on the wall, seemed to glow in the moonlight, like the garb of an angel.

"I found him, Granddaddy," she whispered. "I found the man I know you always wanted for me, and we're going to make a family, right here at Primrose Creek."

There was no reply, of course, but Megan still felt a sense of Gideon McQuarry's presence. He'd be there, the next afternoon, when she and Webb were married, she was sure of that.

Smiling, she closed her eyes and drifted off to sleep.

The new bed felt as if it was an acre across, Webb reflected, as he lay with his hands behind his head, smiling into the darkness. Come tomorrow night, Megan would be there with him, and that would make all the difference.

He wanted her, there was no question of that, and he wanted her soon. But he knew she was going to bring a lot more to his life than pleasure; she already had. She'd brought laughter and hope and feelings

Webb had never experienced. Before she came, his life had stretched before him, vast and empty. Now, it looked like the land of milk and honey.

Saturday morning arrived, right on schedule.

At long, long last, Megan's wedding day had come, and she had the dress and the bridegroom to prove it.

Christy and Bridget and Skye fussed over her happily, upstairs in the room she would share with Webb after that night. Clearly, Caney had not yet told the two elder sisters about their mother; Megan would have been able to see signs of it if she had, and there would not have been this sense of merry chaos.

"You are beautiful," Christy said, and smiled. Her eyes glittered with joy and pride. "It just doesn't seem possible—our little Megan, a bride."

Bridget assessed Megan proudly. She'd arranged her hair, weaving in baby's breath and buttercups, and Skye's contribution was the bouquet of daisies, bluebells, and wild tiger lilies she carried, gathered from the meadow above the stream bank only minutes before. "Lovely," she agreed.

A knock sounded at the bedroom door, and Skye hurried over to open it just a crack, peering out into the hallway. "Webb Stratton, you know perfectly well you aren't allowed to see the bride!" she scolded, but there was a smile in her voice.

"I just wanted to make sure she hadn't climbed out the window and headed for the hills," he replied. "Reverend Taylor's here, by the way, and he keeps pulling out his pocket watch and saying he's got a salvation sermon to give this afternoon."

Skye looked back at Megan, who nodded.

"We'll be right down," she said.

"Bring Megan," Webb replied, and then Megan heard his boot heels on the wooden stairs just down the hall.

"Are you ready?" Christy asked.

Megan nodded. Each of her sisters embraced her, Christy first, then Bridget, then Skye, who threw in a kiss on the cheek for good measure.

"Let's go," Megan said after drawing one more deep breath.

Skye descended the stairs first, then Bridget, then Christy, who was to stand up for Megan as a witness. Megan followed slowly, relishing the moment, wanting this day to last forever. The house gleamed, and the people she loved best in the world were gathered in the parlor, including Caney. Her new husband, Malcolm, stood proudly at her side.

Megan's gaze ricocheted to Webb's face. Standing with Zachary at his right side, he watched her with frank admiration and a sort of wonder that caused her heart to overflow. She loved him. She *loved* him! First chance she got, she'd say so, right out, too. Something that personal had to be said in private, that was all.

Reverend Taylor cleared his throat, and Megan took her place shoulder-to-shoulder with Webb, there in front of the fireplace. The preacher began to read, and Megan answered when she was called upon, her voice whisper-soft. So did Webb, though he sounded gruff instead. He was, Megan suspected, as nervous as she was, and somehow that was comforting.

Finally, the reverend pronounced them man and wife, and Megan was overwhelmed by the enormity of it all. It was a good thing Webb turned and took her into his arms then to kiss her, because she figured she would have swooned dead away if he hadn't been holding on to her.

The touch of his mouth on hers was as gentle as the brush of a feather and, at the same time, as hot as fire. When the kiss ended, she looked up at him, blinking and a little stunned, and everyone else in the wedding party laughed and applauded.

Congratulations rained down on the bride and groom, and there were more hugs, more kisses, more tears and laughter. Megan set her wilting bouquet aside on a table, and Augustus, always one to observe any occasion to excess, snatched it and ran furiously around and around the parlor. Then he dropped the flowers in a colorful tumble at Megan's feet and looked up at her with so much unreserved adoration that she couldn't resist bending down to kiss the top of his furry head and ruffle his silly ears.

When the cake—Bridget's famous recipe with coconut frosting—was served, Megan made sure Augustus got a good-sized piece, like every other guest at the wedding.

It was nearly sunset when the well-wishers left, tearing themselves away, family by family, until Webb and Megan were completely alone.

Webb cupped her chin in one hand. "If it isn't Mrs. Webb Stratton," he said, and grinned. Then he took out his pocket watch, flipped open the case, and considered the time.

"What are you doing?"

"Calculating when our first child will be born. I put it at nine months and two hours."

Megan blushed. "That soon?"

He lifted her up into his arms. "That soon," he confirmed, and headed toward the stairs. Augustus padded after them and whimpered once, disconsolately, when the door of the master bedroom closed in his face.

Chapter

11

"There's something I—I need to tell you," Megan murmured, gazing up into her husband's face as he gently removed the pins from her hair, one by one, and set them atop the bureau. "Before—"

He let her hair fall around his fingers, his hands gently cupping her skull on either side, his callused thumbs tracing the prominent ridges of her cheek-bones. There was a quiet, knowing expression in his eyes. "I'm listening," he said, his voice gruff.

She drew a deep breath, let it out slowly. "I love you."

He was silent for a few moments, apparently absorbing those words, weighing them in his heart and mind. "Now, that's interesting," he said. "I was about to say the same thing to you."

She felt her eyes go wide. He was standing so close that she could feel the heat from his body, sense the strength in his arms and legs and chest. Unlike many men, he never wore oil or pomade in his hair, and he smelled deliciously of pipe smoke, summer winds, and a subtle, teasing scent that might have been store-bought soap or cologne or something entirely his own. "When did you know?" she asked when she could get her tongue to cooperate with the effort.

"Oh, I reckon I've been in love with you right along. I only admitted as much to myself a few days ago, though."

She nodded, shaken and certain that if he weren't resting his hands on her shoulders, she would surely have risen right off the floor, like a stage sprite harnessed to an invisible wire. "I don't exactly know how to do this," she confided, whispering, as though they were in the midst of a crowd instead of their own bedroom, on a ranch several miles from town.

He arched an eyebrow and grinned slightly, gave her shoulders the lightest possible squeeze. "This?" he teased, pretending not to know what she meant.

She swallowed. "Lovemaking," she replied, even more quietly than before.

His brow crumpled, but there was still a blue light dancing in his eyes. "Oh," he said. "I understood you to say you were a woman of experience."

He would find her wanting, she was sure he would, as soon as he discovered how little she knew about the act of love. She was utterly mortified and quite unable to speak.

"Ah," Webb said, as though enlightened by her silence.

She felt her face ignite with embarrassment. "It—it only happened once, and I—well—it was terrible—"

He was combing her hair with his fingers now, and

she felt his breath on her forehead. "Did you feel the way you feel right now?"

She paused, considered the question, and then shook her head. She couldn't have spoken, though; her throat had drawn shut again, like a tobacco pouch with the strings pulled tight.

He smiled, tilted her chin, and looked straight into her eyes. "Let me show you," he said, "how a woman *should* be loved."

A sweet, hard shiver went through her, partly disquiet but mostly anticipation. She nodded, still stricken to silence, to let him know she wasn't scared. She closed her eyes when she felt his hands slide down from her shoulders along her arms to her hands. He raised one to his mouth and brushed the knuckles with his lips, then did the same with the other, taking his time. The very slowness of the gestures stirred exquisite sensations in the most sensitive parts of her body.

After a few delicious moments, he turned her around, so that her back was to him, and began unfastening the cloth buttons that held her wedding gown closed. When the dress was open to the waist, Webb slipped his hands inside, boldly caressing her breasts.

Megan groaned and let her head fall back against Webb's shoulder.

He chuckled, as though amused by her response. It was a heavenly misery, and, to compound matters, he slipped his thumbs inside her camisole, brushing her nipples until they hardened like creek stones. She gasped, and he continued his teasing, bending to kiss her temple and then nibble at her earlobe. By the time he got to her neck, she was dizzy with wanting, but this, she soon discovered, was only the beginning.

While he continued to tease her nipples with one hand, Webb slid the other down over her bare belly, leaving the nerve endings jumping under her skin as he went. He made a circle around her navel, with just the tip of his finger, and continued to nibble and nip at her earlobe. Involuntarily, Megan thrust her hips forward, and that was when he reached beneath the waistline of her petticoat and bloomers and found the warm, moist delta where her thighs met.

She stiffened, her back curved.

"Shhh," he murmured against her ear, and she sagged against him, gave herself up to the fierce pleasure of his touch. Surely, she thought, half-blind with need, it must be a sin to feel like this, to want something—some*one*—so badly.

He eased the dress down over her shoulders and let it fall to the floor in a rustling circle, soft as flower petals. Then, because her knees were threatening to fail her, he curved one arm around her middle and held her against him. Now, in addition to the fury he was stirring with his fingers, she felt the length and heat of him pressing into her lower back. She began to thrust her hips into his hand, seeking something she couldn't have explained.

He kissed her bare shoulders, one and then the other. "Not so fast," he said in a rasp. He turned her to face him once more and began removing his own clothes, his eyes linked with hers the whole time. She ached to have him touch her again but was too proud to say so. Instead, she raised trembling hands to take off her few remaining garments.

She had no memory of lying down on the bed, no idea whether she went under her own power or Webb carried her. She was aware only of her own responses, and of Webb, and of the pinkish-gold light of a fading sun pooling around them.

Webb was naked, and he was glorious. She wanted to touch him everywhere, not only to give him pleasure, though she certainly wanted that, but because he fascinated her. In the combined glow of sunset and her love, he looked like some gilded creature, more of heaven than earth. He was strong, and yet he handled her with infinite tenderness, even reverence.

He kissed her, again and again, and she kissed back. Webb's lovemaking was not something to be endured but something to be reveled in, surrendered to, celebrated. When he cupped one of her breasts in his hand and tasted the nipple, already taut from stroking, Megan arched her back and gave a long, shuddering sigh. Groping, she plunged her fingers into his hair, then let them wander up and down his back in a frantic search.

He moved to her other breast and enjoyed it thoroughly before finding his way to her belly, where he dipped the tip of his tongue into her navel as though he'd found honey there. She shivered again, moaned in her throat.

She thought it was over then, that he would take her, because he moved her knees apart and centered himself between them. She closed her eyes and braced herself for pain, and instead encountered an ecstasy so forbidden that she had never even imagined it before, let alone experienced it. He found her most delicate and private place and took suckle there, on the nubbin of flesh that throbbed against his tongue in frantic welcome.

She cried out, a great, triumphant, groaning shout, and wove her fingers into his hair again, holding him close and closer, even as she tossed her head back and forth on the pillow like a woman in a fever. If he didn't stop, she would die, and if he *did,* she would die. She'd raised herself onto the soles of her feet, seeking him, and he braced his hands under her buttocks and held her high to his mouth. He was insatiable, relentless, and utterly wonderful.

Fierce satisfaction swelled and billowed, swelled and billowed within her, like the sails of a ship catching the wind. On and on it went, while Megan flung back her head and tried to stay with her bucking body. Webb slipped her legs over his shoulders and took her to what was surely the end of the journey. Sobbing, her body still flexing long after all her strength was spent, Megan held nothing back.

It was not the end, she was startled to discover when Webb finally lowered her gently to the bed, but merely the beginning. He lay as close as a second skin, his arms around her, and soothed her while she regained her senses. Then he gently spread her legs again and mounted her, and she was amazed to feel herself catch fire again the instant he entered her. As his thrusts grew more urgent, more powerful, she moved with him, stroking his back, holding his face, drawing him down, again and again, for her kiss.

When release came, it swept them both up into a golden fury, and, for a time, their bodies belonged neither to them as individuals nor to each other but to the same forces that spawned stars and fires, mountains and floods. Megan was flung so far heavenward, so fiercely, that she never expected to return from the skies and be herself again.

After several such encounters, sleep finally claimed the lovers, and when Megan awakened in the morning, she was alone in their marriage bed. She sat upright, unaccountably frightened that Webb had abandoned her, but he was standing at one of the windows, hands braced against the sill, gazing out. He wore trousers and boots, but his chest was bare, and his suspenders dangled below his hips. Megan thought he looked delicious.

"Good morning, Mr. Stratton," she said, stretching.

He turned his head, grinned at her. "Don't tempt me," he warned. "I might just come back to bed and have my way with you."

Megan did not lower her arms. Although she was covered by the top sheet, she was naked underneath, and, of course, Webb knew that. "Do you suppose we've started that baby?" she asked, batting her lashes once or twice. She knew they were thick, and one of her best features.

He crossed to her, leaned down, and placed a noisy kiss on her mouth. "Stop it," he growled. "I've got a ranch to run. I can't be lolling around in bed with my wife all day."

She slipped her arms around his neck. "Can't you just—loll—for a little while?"

He laughed. "No," he answered firmly. He touched the tip of her nose with an index finger. "Tonight, however, is another matter." With that, he tugged down the sheet, took a leisurely sip at each of her breasts, and then left her to contemplate her situation.

She got up, muttering, and hastily washed and dressed. Webb had already started breakfast when she got downstairs, and Augustus, waiting for his share of the sausage and the eggs from Bridget's chickens, spared her only a single glance, the ingrate. Apparently, he'd already forgotten the piece of wedding cake she'd given him.

"Shall I bring dinner up to the meadow?" she asked Webb. Although the sun was up, it was still very early, and there was a kerosene lantern burning in the middle of the table. It gave the room a cozy glow, as did the small fire Webb had built on the hearth, and Megan felt sinfully contented.

Webb gave her a sidelong glance, skillfully turning sizzling sausage patties in the big iron pan. "The men have probably got a rabbit stew or a pot of beans on the fire," he said. "Why don't you just spend today resting up for tonight?"

Megan moved behind her husband, slipped her arms around his waist, let her cheek rest in the space between his shoulder blades. He'd put on one of the shirts she'd sewed for him, and she could smell his singular scent through the cloth. "You *are* confident," she said, and laughed softly.

He turned, drew her close, kissed her. "Last night, you seemed to think that confidence was justified," he drawled. "If I remember correctly, you were tearing my hair and sobbing and pleading for more."

It was all true, of course, but it was insufferable of

him to remind her in the broad light of day. "Webb Stratton!" she gasped, mortified and flattered and excited, all of a piece.

"Just wait until tonight," he said, and when, laughing, she flailed at him with both fists, he grasped her wrists and subdued her with a kiss that left her sagging against him. Then he swatted her bottom, seated her at the table, and served her breakfast.

Christy and Bridget sat in Bridget's parlor, their eyes swollen, hankies clutched in their hands. "They've been this way for days," Skye confided in a theatrical whisper. Megan had been married a full month, and well occupied most of that time. Now, seeing the state her sisters were in, she felt guilty for being so happy.

"Caney told them," Megan guessed.

Skye's brown eyes widened. "You *knew*? About Diamond Lil and—and our papa?"

Megan nodded, then sighed. "Lillian told me the day I went to see her about our partnership."

"*And you didn't say anything?*" Skye hissed.

Both Christy and Bridget were glaring at her accusingly, and Megan realized that they had overheard. She straightened her spine, squared her shoulders, and marched across the room to stand between their two chairs. She rested her hands on her hips, feeling very matronly now that she was an old married woman of thirty days. "Stop feeling sorry for yourselves," she said crisply. "You're a disgrace, the pair of you!"

For once in their lives, her elder sisters were speechless.

"Your mother is alive." She gestured wildly with one

hand in the general direction of town. "She's barely two miles from here. Don't you have questions you want to ask her? Don't you have things you want to say?"

Bridget's jawline tightened. "You bet your bustle I do," she said, rising out of her chair, then sitting down again.

"Well?" Skye prompted, spreading her hands.

Bridget's lower lip wobbled, but only slightly. Her posture was as proud as ever. "I'm not sure where to start."

"Start?" Christy whispered miserably, and dabbed at her eyes again with a wadded handkerchief. "Our mother is a *prostitute*. That's not a beginning, it's an end!"

"Oh, for heaven's sake," Megan said. "There are worse things, you know."

"What?" Christy sniffled, plainly mystified.

"What if she'd kept you? Raised you in a series of saloons and brothels? She cared enough to give you both up, to give you a family and a good home," Megan said, losing patience. Always the youngest, the pet of the family, she wasn't used to taking charge in moments of crisis. She rather liked it. "Do stop behaving like a pair of babies!"

"I'm going to town to speak to my mother," Bridget said decisively, rising again, looking down at a profoundly stunned Christy, who was still in her chair. "Are you coming or not?"

Never one to be bested, even at something she didn't want to do in the first place, Christy bolted to her feet. "Of course I am," she replied. Then Bridget turned to Megan and Skye.

"Will you please look after the children?" she asked.

Megan nodded. Since Christy had brought little Joseph and Margaret along to this crying fest, all the kids were close at hand.

The two daughters of Lillian Colefield did not trouble themselves with a change of clothes, nor did they splash their faces with cold water or attend to their hair. No, they crossed the bridge over the creek in single file, then set out for town, arm in arm, like a two-woman army marching on an unsuspecting city.

"You suppose they'll be all right?" Skye asked, peering after their sisters as they ascended the steep bank on the other side of Primrose Creek.

"I'm more worried about anybody who might get in their way," Megan replied, and laughed. The morning was a happy one, spent playing games in the yard with the nieces and nephews, and when Bridget and Christy returned, after two hours, they were dry-eyed and introspective. Neither of them wanted to give an account of their interview with Diamond Lil, and Megan and Skye weren't foolish enough to ask. In fact, they wisely took their leave, Skye with her two children, Megan with Augustus, who had come to escort his mistress back along the creek path. She was pleased by his attentions, as always, and stopped several times to throw a stick and then praise him outlandishly for fetching.

She was smiling when she rounded the last bend and saw the familiar horse standing in the dooryard, reins dangling. Webb was home.

Augustus ran to his master, barking with glee, and Webb laughed as he bent down to ruffle the animal's loose, gleaming hide.

"You're back early," Megan commented, quite unnecessarily. She was Webb's bride, and she shared his bed, and still her heart leaped every time she laid eyes on him, whether close up or from a distance.

He straightened, grinning. "I got to hankering for my wife," he said.

Megan bit her lower lip and waited.

He extended a hand, and she crossed the distance between them without further hesitation. He kissed the backs of her knuckles, one by one, sending hot shivers throughout her body. Then he whisked her up into his arms and carried her not toward the house, as she had expected, but in the direction of the barn.

"What—?" she managed.

He gave her a long, deep kiss, without slackening his pace. "There are a thousand places I mean to have you," he said when at last he raised his mouth from hers, "and the hayloft is one of them."

The inside of the barn was cool and shadowy, rife with the scents of animals and hay and saddle leather. Augustus, by that time, had lost interest in the activities of his master and mistress and trotted off on some errand of his own.

Webb set Megan on her feet in front of the ladder leading up into the loft. She met his eyes, briefly, and then began to climb.

Chapter

12

$\mathcal{M}$egan stood in the dooryard, watching as the woman drove the livery rig, a dusty buggy, deftly across the shallow creek. There was a young, fair-haired boy on the seat beside her, about the same age as Bridget's Noah and Skye's Hank. Even from that distance, Megan somehow knew that the child's eyes would be periwinkle-blue.

As the wayfarers drew nearer, Megan could see that the woman was like a cameo come to life. Her skin was a flawless shade of ivory, her eyes some dark shade of purple or brown. *Ellie*, Megan thought, full of amazement and despair.

In her spotless traveling suit, made of lightweight, cream-colored linen, Ellie Stratton made Megan feel as though she'd stitched all her own garments together from potato sacks. She'd been meaning to sew some new dresses, but, what with one thing and another, she just hadn't had time.

The other Mrs. Stratton drew back on the reins and

smiled, though there was a certain caution lurking in her eyes, as though she might be unsure of her welcome. "I guess you must be Megan," she said.

Megan barely returned the smile, and she could only speculate about what was visible in her own eyes. She felt such a tangle of things, she couldn't begin to sort them out. Unfortunately, Christian charity wasn't among them. Whatever Ellie Stratton wanted, she'd been Webb's first love, and Megan dreaded seeing them together. "Hullo, Mrs. Stratton," she replied.

Ellie winced slightly. Augustus had ambled over to investigate, and the boy was looking at him with interest. Interest and those blue-purple eyes Megan had been so certain he would have. "Just call me Ellie," she said. "If you wouldn't mind."

Megan nodded and then smiled at the boy, who was still watching Augustus with fascination. "He's friendly," she said. "You can pet him if it's all right with your mother."

"Go ahead, Tommy," Ellie told the boy.

Tommy climbed nimbly down and put out a tentative hand to Augustus. The dog responded with a long slurp of his tongue, and a delighted laugh bubbled from the little boy. Ellie alighted, much more gracefully than her son had done, and stood facing Megan.

"You're just as pretty as Jesse said you were," Ellie said. "Is—is Webb at home, by any chance?"

Megan was about to say that he wasn't, when they all turned at the sound of a rider coming across the creek. It was Webb.

Megan's knees nearly buckled with relief at the mere sight of him, but, at the same time, she feared the moment when he recognized Ellie, the woman he'd once wanted for his wife, and the boy.

Ellie was on her way to him even before he'd reached the yard. When he swung down from the saddle and embraced her, she put her arms around his neck.

Megan stood rigid, watching. Waiting. She was only vaguely aware of the boy and dog, now running round and round in a huge circle, both of them barking.

Ellie and Webb parted, but she was beaming up into his face. Her joy in seeing him would have been obvious to anyone, although Webb's state of mind was not so easy to read. He took her elbow in one hand and started toward Megan, leading the horse along behind.

Megan called upon all her theatrical ability just to smile.

"I guess you've met my brother's wife," Webb said. Was she mistaken, or had he put a slight emphasis on the last three words?

"And I've met Megan," Ellie said, as though it were the most natural thing in the world for a first love to come calling at the hot tail end of a July afternoon. She gestured for the boy to come to her side, and he obeyed, albeit with reluctance. Seeing him with Webb took Megan's breath away, so great was the resemblance. "Tommy, this is your Uncle Webb."

Webb crouched, facing the child. "Hullo, Tommy," he said.

"Hullo," Tommy replied uncertainly. He might have moved a fraction of an inch closer to his mother, though there was no telling for sure.

Webb stood up, and his gaze caught Megan's and held on. No smile. "Let's all go inside," he said.

Megan knew her fears were irrational, for the most part, but that didn't stop the inward shiver that coursed through her just then. Was Webb going to tell her that this was his boy, his and Ellie's? The resemblance was amazing, but then, Jesse looked very much like Webb. Perhaps Tom Jr. did, too.

They entered through the main door, and Megan immediately made for the kitchen. She put on a pot of coffee and cut slices from a pan of yellow cake she'd baked earlier to serve at supper. She set a plate on the floor for an appreciative Augustus and put three others on an old cupboard door that she liked to use as a tray.

Webb was seated in his chair near the fire, the very place where he'd often said, jokingly, that he meant to pass his old age. Ellie and Tommy sat side by side on the settee, and Ellie's feelings for Webb were evident in her eyes in a way they had not been before. Try though she might, Megan still couldn't make sense of Webb's expression; it was closed, unreadable.

"Never mind the coffee," he said when Megan had set down the tray and started back toward the kitchen. "Sit down and catch your breath."

Catch your breath. Megan wasn't so sure she was ever going to breathe easily again—not, at least, while Ellie Stratton was there in her parlor, making cow eyes at *her* husband. Megan sat and took some pleasure in the fact that her chair was the mate to Webb's, and close enough that she could have reached out a hand to touch his arm or his knee.

All the same, her heart was pounding.

Ellie fiddled with the drawstring bag in her lap and brought out a sheaf of papers. She leaned over to hand them to Webb, and, although the move could not have been described as coquettish, it nonetheless made Megan want to pull out the other woman's hair.

Silently, she instructed herself not to be such a ninny, but it didn't do much good where her feelings were concerned.

Webb took the papers, unfolded them, scanned the words therein. Megan saw his jawline tighten.

"I'm sorry to tell you this way," Ellie said gently. "Your pa died six months ago. Tom Jr. took over the Southern Star, but one third of it is yours, and one third is Jesse's. We didn't know where you were till Jesse came home."

Webb handed back the papers. "They can split the difference," he said. "Tom Jr. and Jesse. I've got a ranch of my own, right here."

Megan wondered if the dizzying range of emotions she was feeling showed in her face or countenance, but since no one but Augustus was looking at her anyway, she guessed it didn't matter.

"I'm afraid it isn't that easy," Ellie replied. "The will is written in such a way that if one son refuses his share, the other two lose theirs as well. And on top of that, you have to live there, all three of you, and work the place the way your father did."

Webb got up and turned his back to stand at the front window, looking out at the land he loved as much as Megan did. He'd poured a lot of himself into making that ranch what it was. "They can fight that in court, break the will. Tom Jr. and Jesse, I mean. It's unreasonable to insist that we all live there."

Ellie's face was filled with pain and memories of

pain. "Yes, it's unreasonable. That was your father, in a word." She paused, murmured to the boy that he ought to go and eat his cake on the stoop, which he gratefully did, and then went on with a sort of despairing tenacity. "Tom Jr. won't last the year, Webb. The doctor says his liver has been eating itself away for a decade. Jesse can't handle that place on his own; he's too young. So even if they convinced a judge—"

Megan watched, her heart pounding so loud she was sure it must be audible, as Webb turned from the window. With both his elder brother and his father gone, Webb might well want to return to the Southern Star. After all, he'd been born on that ranch, and his mother was buried there. Perhaps that was home to him, not Primrose Creek.

"What about you and the boy, Ellie?" Webb asked. "What's your place in all this?"

What, indeed? Megan wondered, and hoped nobody had noticed that she was sitting on the edge of her chair.

Ellie lowered her head for a moment, and when she looked up, her eyes were shimmering with tears. Crying always made Megan look puffy and mottled, with her delicate redhead's coloring, but this woman managed to weep gracefully. She might have been a fallen goddess, wrongfully toppled from her pedestal in some pagan temple. "I told Tom Jr. that Tommy and I wouldn't stay around and watch him drink himself to death, and I meant it."

Megan closed her eyes tightly, braced herself. Ellie had come searching for the brother she truly loved, and the boy would probably provide any further inducement that might be necessary.

"What do you mean to do, then?" Webb wanted to know. Megan could not tell anything at all from his tone, but when she realized he was standing behind her chair, when she felt his hand come to rest lightly on her shoulder, a jolt went through her.

Ellie's gaze was steady. Level. "We'll get to that later," she said, showing the tensile strength underlaying her nature. "Right now, I'm trying to protect my son's future. Tom Sr.'s will is specific. If Tom Jr. dies, the ranch becomes yours and Jesse's, in equal shares. You'll still have to live on the land, both of you. If one of you chooses not to accept the terms, then, like I said, the property will be forfeited. If that happens, of course, then Tommy will have nothing when he comes of age."

Megan felt chilled through and through, and her stomach was jumpy. She was glad she hadn't tried to eat any cake, because she might have disgraced herself by clapping one hand over her mouth and running out of the room.

"That mean old son-of-a-bitch," Webb murmured. "God in heaven. The man's dead and buried, and he's still trying to run all our lives."

"My family isn't wealthy, Webb," Ellie said. "A share of that ranch is all Tommy will ever have."

Webb sighed. "He looks like a sturdy little fella. I imagine you're underestimating him, Ellie." He squeezed Megan's shoulder once more, reassuring her only slightly, then turned and walked back to his desk. She heard him pull back the chair and sit down, knew he was reading his father's will in depth this time, word by word.

"I'll get that coffee," Megan said, and bolted, because she couldn't stand the tension anymore, couldn't bear just sitting there, with everything she cared about hanging in the balance.

"I don't want any, thank you!" Ellie called after her, and Megan already knew that Webb would refuse a cup, but she went about the task anyway because it gave her something to do with her hands, and she sorely needed that.

Minutes later, standing in the kitchen doorway watching Tommy and Augustus bounding tirelessly about the yard, Megan heard Webb and Ellie talking, their voices rapid and earnest. She couldn't make out the words, but the tones said a lot, Ellie's high and timorous, Webb's low and hoarse. Despair filled Megan, as though she were flooded to the neck with brackish water.

Presently, Ellie appeared, her eyes showing evidence of more exquisitely lovely tears, her chin high. She nodded to Megan, as cordially as she could, and stepped past her into the yard. "Come along, Tommy," she called. "We'll miss the stagecoach to Virginia City."

Tommy waved to Megan and to Webb, who was standing silently behind her, but his most sincere farewell went to Augustus. Ellie climbed gracefully into the buggy and took up the reins without looking in their direction at all, waited for her son, and drove away.

"You're going," Megan said, without turning around to face her husband.

"I have to," he replied, and walked away.

Megan stood on the threshold for a long time, hug-

ging herself, struggling not to cry. Damn Webb
Stratton, anyway, if that was all their marriage meant
to him. She'd get along just fine without him.

When she went upstairs, not bothering with supper,
Webb was at his desk in the parlor, wearing his reading
spectacles and going over a stack of ledgers and loose
papers. He looked up when she paused on the first
landing, and their gazes locked, but neither of them
spoke.

It was late when he came to bed, but Megan had not
slept. She wasn't sure she would ever sleep again.

"Why?" she asked. Despite the spareness of the
question, he knew full well what she meant.

He sighed. "Because of the boy."

Her heart turned brittle and trembled, on the verge
of shattering. "Yes," she said. "Because of the boy."

Webb spoke gently, in a hoarse voice. "He's my
nephew, Megan," he said. "Not my son. But whatever
my differences with the kid's father, I can't just turn
my back and let him lose everything. I feel some
responsibility toward Jesse, too."

Did he expect her to be reasonable? She couldn't,
not where their parting was concerned. She said nothing.

Webb knew she was crying, of course, since the bed
was shaking. He turned her into his arms, pulled her
against his chest. "I'll sell off the herd," he said, "and
you can stay in town or with one of your sisters. There's
enough money to see you through—"

She pushed away from him. "No, Webb," she
replied tartly. "If I can't go with you, and I suspect I
won't be invited, then I'm not leaving this ranch. You

promised to sign the place over to me if anything happened to—to us, remember?"

His sigh was gusty, a raw sound, fraught with pain. "It's a long, dangerous trip from here to Montana, Megan."

She turned her back again, and this time, he didn't touch her. "Not too long and dangerous for Ellie, I see," she said, and hated herself for jealousy so evident in her voice. "Well, I'll have you know, Webb Stratton, that I traveled to and from England on a small ship without any trouble at all." *Other than a week of seasickness each way,* chided a voice in her mind. "Furthermore, I came west with Caney and Christy in a wagon, and we ran into just about every hardship a body can come up against."

"Ellie made the trip for her son."

"She made the trip for you," Megan insisted, and Webb did not deny that. In fact, he was typically straightforward.

"She hoped Jesse had been mistaken about my marrying you, that there might be a chance for her and me once Tom Jr. passes. I told her different."

"But you're leaving with her."

"No, Megan. She and the boy are going back east to live with her folks. I'm headed up to Montana to work this whole thing through with my brothers. I'll be back in a few months, I promise."

Megan felt both relief and doubt. Relief because she knew Webb didn't make promises lightly, and doubt because nobody was more aware than she was of the bonds between family members. "I don't believe you."

He chuckled, but there was no humor in the sound. "That's apparent," he said. Then he stroked the length of her side with his left hand, and, in complete contrast to her emotions, a rush of need went through her, powerful as a flash flood spilling into a dry creekbed.

Against her will, against her better judgment, she turned to him, this man who was leaving her. This man who might never be back, no matter what he said to the contrary.

Their lovemaking was fierce that night, a thing of sorrow as much as passion, a holding on and a letting go. Even as her body spasmed with almost unbearable pleasure, Megan sobbed.

The next day, Webb went to town and came back with a paper transferring ownership of the ranch at Primrose Creek into Megan's name, along with an envelope full of money drawn on his account at the bank. They didn't speak all day, except in broken sentences, and poor Augustus, sensing that something fundamental had shifted, was beside himself. That night in bed, however, Webb and Megan made love as wildly, as desperately, as they had the night before. It was almost a form of combat rather than communion, but it was no less satisfying for that. Megan knew Webb was as deeply affected as she was, but none of that made any difference. Webb was leaving, and soon, and Megan grew more convinced with every passing moment that he wouldn't return. She'd already suffered too much loss to believe in happy endings where things like that were concerned.

On the third day after Megan's world cracked down the middle and began to come apart, Webb arranged

by wire to sell the cattle to the army at far less than the
going price, and he managed to hire enough men to
help drive the beasts as far as Fort Grant. He would
ride on from there alone.

It would have changed everything if he'd taken her
with him, but he wasn't going to do that, and she
wasn't being given a say in the matter. She might have
followed Webb, forced him either to take her along or
waste time doubling back to bring her home again, but
she had a very personal and private reason for not
doing that.

So she tried to resign herself to losing the only man
she would ever love.

On the morning Webb left, with all his cattle and a
half-dozen cowhands, Megan stood at the edge of the
high meadow, watching. Augustus, confused, ran fran-
tically back and forth between Webb's horse and
Megan, yipping sorrowfully.

"Go on home, boy," Webb said to him. "Go home
with Megan."

Megan was blind with tears when the dog trotted
back to her, glancing over his shoulder, once or twice,
lest Webb summon him, as he came. She couldn't
wave; she couldn't even find the strength to say good-
bye. So she just stood there, like a tree stump, and
watched as Webb rode away.

Soon, there was nothing left to see but a roiling
cloud of dust in the distance, nothing left to hear but
the incessant bawling of all those cattle. Megan turned,
a whimpering Augustus at her side, and made her way
back down the hill and along an old trail toward the
house.

She stood in the dooryard for a while, looking around her at the land her Granddaddy had left her. She'd gotten what she wanted—it was hers again, and hers alone, and she would never let it go.

Drying her eyes on the hem of her apron, she went inside to put on a pot of tea.

Fat flakes of snow drifted past the window over the kitchen work table, and Caney, spreading slices of dried apple in a pie shell, turned with a beaming smile to Megan. "The young'uns will love this," she said. "They always like a good snow."

Megan, kneading bread at the table near the fire, smiled. "Trace made them all sleds," she said, referring to the many cousins living up and down Primrose Creek. "They'll be looking for a slippery hill."

Caney's expression turned somber. She was well along with her and Malcolm's first child, and pregnancy had rendered her more exotically beautiful than ever before. "You hear anything from Webb?" she asked in a small voice.

Megan figured her sisters had probably put Caney up to asking the question, since she'd made it clear she didn't want to discuss the matter with them. She'd had two letters from him in the months he'd been gone, one saying that Tom Jr. had died and he and Jesse were trying to sort things through with a pack of lawyers, the other containing a bank draft and a promise, neither of which carried much weight with Megan by that time. She hadn't written him back, because she couldn't do that without telling him about the baby, and she wasn't about to beg or use weakness to get what she wanted.

Caney abandoned her pie-making and crossed the room to take Megan into her arms. Their protruding stomachs bounced against each other, and both women laughed, though Megan had already given way to tears. Kindness always did that to her, always broke down her defenses.

"If I didn't have this here baby in me," Caney said, rocking Megan back and forth the way she'd done for years and years, "I declare I'd go find that man and take a horsewhip to him."

Megan sniffled, straightened her spine, and dashed at her cheek with the back of one hand. "If he doesn't want me and our baby, then we don't want him, either. I'll hire somebody to run this ranch and go to work for Lil in her new show house."

Caney put a finger under Megan's chin and lifted. "Does Webb even know about this chile, girl? Or were you too proud to tell him?"

Megan used her apron to mop her face, which was as wet as if she'd stuck her whole head into a pail of water. She had suspected her condition before Webb left for Montana, but she hadn't said a word. "I couldn't," she said. "And it isn't a matter of pride, Caney. He would have stayed—yes, I'm sure he would have stayed—but against his will and for all the wrong reasons."

"He got a right to know, Megan," Caney insisted. "Might be growin' inside you, but that babe belongs to him, too."

"I'll tell him—sometime," she said.

Caney made a clucking sound with her tongue and shook her head. "I think you ought to write him. I'll leave the letter off for mailin' when I get back to town."

Megan shook her head. Then she turned her back, went to the basin, and thoroughly washed not only her hands but her tear-stained face, too. That done, she went back to the table, put the dough into buttered pans, and set it to rise on a table near the hearth.

Caney was still working on her pies—they were having a family dinner that night, at Bridget's to celebrate Noah's birthday—when all of a sudden she let out a long, low whistle and crowed right out loud. Augustus got up from his rug in front of the fire and gave a lazy *woof, woof*.

Caney turned, gesturing wildly, her face wreathed in a glorious smile. "Git over here, girl, and look out this winder!" she cried.

Frowning, her heart picking up speed, Megan obeyed, wiping her hands on a dish towel as she went. When she reached the window, looked out, and saw a man on horseback crossing the creek, she drew in her breath. Although the horse, a strawberry roan, was unfamiliar, and the rider wore a long coat and a hat with a wide brim pulled down low against the freezing wind, Megan knew him instantly, and her heart rushed out to meet him.

"Webb," she whispered.

"Speak of the devil," Caney cried joyously, raising both hands into the air and shaking them in a sort of unspoken hallelujah. Immediately, she bustled over, took her cloak down from one of the row of pegs next to the door, and put it on. "I got me news to pass!"

Megan didn't even think about a coat. She just

opened the door and stepped out into the snowy chill, barely noticing when Caney tried to pull her back. Augustus dashed by, a golden streak shooting across the snow, barking so hard he was bound to be hoarse come morning.

Webb rode to the middle of the yard and climbed down. The dog jumped up, his forefeet resting on his master's chest. Webb laughed and ruffled the animal's sides with gloved hands, but his eyes rose to rest on Megan.

"Lord o'mercy," Caney clucked, tucking a cloak around Megan, "you'll catch your death. Then what good will it be, your man comin' home at long last?" She glared at Webb. " 'Bout time," she snapped. Then stomped off through the rising snow in an energetic huff. Just like that, she collected her mule and rode off.

Webb didn't speak, and neither did Megan. She just stood there, afraid to believe he was really back, not an apparition or a figure in a dream. How many nights had she tossed in her lonely bed in the spare room, unable to sleep in the one they had shared, dreaming just this dream? How many times had she awakened, already weeping because she knew it wasn't real?

He faced her, laid his hands on either side of her huge belly. "When?"

"February," she managed to say.

A grin broke across his wind-chapped face. He needed a bath and a shave and a thorough barbering, and he was the most beautiful sight Megan had ever seen. "Guess I got here just in time," he said.

"You're back to stay?" She hardly dared put the question, the answer was so important.

He nodded. "If you'll have me. I settled my business up in Montana, just like I said I would, and now I'm home for good." He propelled her toward the house. "Go on inside before you take a chill. Caney'll have my hide if you do."

She hesitated, then nodded and obeyed, but she stood at a side window, still wearing her cloak, and watched as he led his horse into the barn, watched till he came out again and started toward the house. Only then was she truly convinced that she wasn't imagining everything.

He saw her, grinned.

Her heart tumbled end over end, like a circus acrobat doing somersaults.

He came in, pulled off his gloves, removed his coat and hat, and hung them up like he always had, then moved toward her. "If I can't hold you in my arms, Megan, and lay you down in our bed, I don't know that I'll live much longer. I've missed you so much."

"Whose fault is that?" she demanded, but she was weakening, and he knew it.

"Mine," he said. Then he held out one hand to her. She took it.

He led her inside, lifted her off her feet, and carried her up the stairs, along the hallway, and into their bedroom. The room was cold, going unused the way it had, and once they had divested each other of their clothes, they scrambled under the covers.

Webb slipped beneath the blankets to caress

Megan's stomach, to kiss and nibble at her flesh. Then he was between her legs, parting her, slipping his hands under her bottom. When he tasted her, she cried out. When he indulged, she all but lost her mind. At last, she reached a crescendo that flung her mind in one direction and her spirit in another, and she sank, whimpering, to the mattress.

He murmured to her, kissed her all over. By the time he reached her mouth, she was desperate again. The instant he slid inside her, with touching care, she exploded in satisfaction, but his appeasement took a while. When it overtook him, he stiffened upon her, shuddered violently, and groaned her name like a dying man crying out to heaven.

He fell beside her, and they lay in exhausted silence for a long time, arms and legs entwined, while shadows crept across the room.

"You won't be going back to Montana?" Megan ventured presently. She had to know.

"Maybe for a visit sometime," Webb answered. "Jesse's got a good foreman, though. He'll make a go of the place."

"So the two of you managed to have your father's will overturned?"

Webb sighed. "Yeah," he said. "But the old man didn't make it easy. That's why I was gone so long—there was a lot of wrangling to be done."

Megan snuggled closer still and traced a finger tip down the middle of Webb's bare chest. "If you were a gentleman," she said, "you'd get up and build a fire."

He moved under the blankets again, began kissing her belly. "Who said I was a gentleman?" he countered, his voice muffled. He found her breasts, nibbled at one peak as though it were some delectable delicacy. "Besides, I think things are getting pretty hot right here in this bed. We've got a fire going already, Mrs. Stratton."

She couldn't disagree.

Soon, in fact, she couldn't speak at all.

Epilogue

There they are, my beautiful granddaughters—fiery Bridget, face glowing in the firelight, plainly adoring her husband and that pack of rascally children she and Trace have produced. I well recall the day Trace Qualtrough came to Primrose Creek, on foot and carrying a worn-out saddle over one shoulder, meaning to look after his best friend's widow. They've made them a place to be proud of, since then.

Then there's Christy. She presented the greatest challenge to my matchmaking skills, setting her cap for Jake Vigil the way she did, when it was really young Zachary Shaw, the marshal, she was meant to marry. Things have certainly come right in the end, though not without considerable doing on my part. There are two perfect children in that family, with another on the way, though Christy and Zachary don't suspect it yet.

And Skye. My brave, lovely Skye. She's met her match in Jake Vigil, and between the two of them, they'll build an empire. No, sir, I've got no worries where they're concerned. Their love is as sturdy as the trees bristling on these hills.

Finally, little Megan. Of course, she's not so little anymore—a grown woman, in point of fact—and a beauty into the bargain, with that glorious red hair of hers. She and Webb, they're as well suited as me and my Rebecca were, and that's saying something. Megan's baby will be a girl, as beautiful as her mama, and just as smart and spirited, too. Fact is, they'll have them a flock of girls, the Strattons will, with a couple of boys coming along later, to bring up the rear.

There's snow falling outside, coming down soft and pretty from a heavy sky. Noah, Bridget's boy, he's just about ready to come unstrung, he's so excited about his birthday. He'll grow into a fine man, though not without giving his folks a gray hair or two in the process. Makes me smile to think about it.

Here are Caney Blue and her fine bridegroom, arriving late for the festivities. Happiness has been a long time coming to Caney, and to her husband, too, but they've finally reached a place of peace and plenty, these two good people. Caney's baby girl will grow up right here, with the rest of them.

Darned if Lillian Colefield herself didn't just follow Caney and Malcolm into the house. She's worn pretty well over the years, given all she's gone through. I never expected to see her again, but things do have a way of coming full circle, especially in matters of the heart. I'm glad they've all found each other. Glad I can go now, and meet up with my Rebecca.

She's been waiting a long time.

**COMPLETE YOUR
PRIMROSE COLLECTION.**

Available from
New York Times
bestselling author

Linda Lael Miller

*The Women
of Primrose Creek*

Bridget   Skye

Megan   Christy

POCKET BOOKS

Visit the Simon & Schuster
romance web site:

www.SimonSaysLove.com

and sign up for our
romance e-mail updates!

Keep up on the latest
new romance releases,
author appearances, news, chats,
special offers, and more!
We'll deliver the information
right to your inbox—if it's new,
you'll know about it.

POCKET BOOKS

Return to
a time of romance...

**SONNET
BOOKS**

Where today's

hottest romance authors

bring you vibrant

and vivid love stories

with a dash of history.

PUBLISHED BY POCKET BOOKS